TOUSSAINT L'OUVERTURE

Fighting for Haitian Independence

REBELS WITH A CAUSE

TOUSSAINT L'OUVERTURE

Fighting for Haitian Independence

Richard Worth

Enslow Publishing
101 W. 23rd Street
Suite 240
New York, NY 10011
USA
enslow.com

Published in 2018 by Enslow Publishing, LLC.
101 W. 23rd Street, Suite 240, New York, NY 10011
Copyright © 2018 by Enslow Publishing, LLC.

Library of Congress Cataloging-in-Publication Data

Names: Worth, Richard, author.
Title: Toussaint L'Ouverture : fighting for Haitian independence / Richard Worth.
Description: New York, NY : Enslow Publishing, [2018] | Series: Rebels with a
cause | Includes bibliographical references and index. | Audience: Grades 7-12.
Identifiers: LCCN 2017003105 | ISBN 9780766085213 (library-bound)
Subjects: LCSH: Toussaint Louverture, 1743-1803—Juvenile literature.. |
Haiti—History—Revolution, 1791-1804—Juvenile literature. |
Revolutionaries—Haiti--Biography--Juvenile literature. |
Generals—Haiti—Biography—Juvenile literature. |
Hait—History—Revolution, 1791-1804—Juvenile literature.
Classification: LCC F1923.T69 W67 2018 | DDC 972.94/03092 [B]—dc23
LC record available at https://lccn.loc.gov/2017003105

Printed in the United States of America

To Our Readers: We have done our best to make sure all website addresses in this
book were active and appropriate when we went to press. However, the author
and the publisher have no control over and assume no liability for the material
available on those websites or on any websites they may link to. Any comments or
suggestions can be sent by email to customerservice@enslow.com.

Photo Credits: Cover, p. 3 Universal History Archive/Universal Images Group/
Getty Images; pp. 7, 16–17, 63, 101 Print Collector/Hulton Archive/Getty Images;
p. 11 Photo12/Universal Images Group/Getty Images; p. 13 Universal Images
Group/Getty Images; p. 15 Buyenlarge/Archive Photos/Getty Images; p. 23 Imagno/
Hulton Fine Art Collection/Getty Images; pp. 26–27 Hulton Archive/Getty Images;
pp. 30, 77, 97 Corbis Historical/Getty Images; pp. 32–33 DEA/G. Dagli Orti/
DeAgostini/Getty Images; p. 39 MPI/Hulton Royals Collection/Getty Images;
p. 42 PHAS/Universal Images Group/Getty Images; p. 44 Photo © Gerald
Bloncourt/Bridgeman Images/Bridgeman Images; p. 47 Bibliotheque Nationale,
Paris, France/Archives Charmet/Bridgeman Images; pp. 50–51, 59 Bettmann/Getty
Images; pp. 54–55 Musee de la Ville de Paris, Musee Carnavalet, Paris, France/
Archives Charmet/Bridgeman Images; p. 65 INTERFOTO/Alamy Stock Photo;
p. 69 Stefano Bianchetti/Corbis Historical/Getty Images; p. 72 Ken Welsh/
Bridgeman Images; p. 81 Archives Charmet/Bridgeman Images; p. 85 DEA Picture
Library/De Agostini/Getty Images; pp. 88–89 DEA/M. Seemuller/De Agostini/
Getty Images; pp. 104–105 GraphicaArtis/Archive Photos/Getty Images; p. 109
Private Collection/Bridgeman Images; interior pages borders, pp. 6–7 background
Eky Studio/Shutterstock.com.

CONTENTS

Introduction................................ 6

1 The Black Spartacus 10

2 Toussaint and Saint-Domingue.... 15

3 Big Whites and Small Whites 29

4 Winds of Change................... 38

5 Slave Revolt in Saint-Domingue .. 46

6 1793–1794 58

7 Slaves No More 68

8 Toussaint in Power................ 76

9 Toussaint Battles Napoleon 84

10 The Final Struggle for Freedom ... 96

Conclusion 108

Chronology............................112

Chapter Notes 115

Glossary 119

Further Reading 121

Index 123

INTRODUCTION

Slavery is almost as old as civilization itself. When a conquering army subdued a city or empire, it generally sold the inhabitants into slavery. In the Old Testament of the Bible, the Jews were conquered and became slaves of the Egyptians, eventually being led out of slavery by Moses. As the Roman Empire conquered the peoples of Europe, the defeated soldiers were paraded in front of the populace in Rome, before being sold into slavery. By the first century AD, Italy had approximately three million slaves, about one-third of the entire population.

In medieval times, Northmen invaded Europe where they captured and enslaved men and women. Meanwhile, across the Middle East, the rise of Islam had led to the conquest of North Africa and Spain. Many thousands of people were enslaved by the conquering armies of Islam, and Muslim merchants sold these slaves throughout the Mediterranean world as well as across Africa. The slave trade also flourished during the fifteenth and sixteenth centuries as first the Portuguese, followed by the British,

Soon after Christopher Columbus visited the island of Hispaniola in 1492, the Spanish began to establish sugar plantations, worked by African slaves.

French, and Dutch, joined the lucrative business of the slave trade. Slaves were captured by warring African tribes and then sold to European merchants who had established forts on the western coast of Africa. These traders then took the slaves to the Caribbean where they were sold to plantation owners or gold and silver mine operators.

When the gold and silver ran out, another form of gold took its place. These were the rich sugar plantations on islands such as Jamaica, Barbados, and Hispaniola.

Sugar plantations of 750 acres (304 hectares) or more were quite common in the Caribbean with more than one hundred slaves on each plantation who did the planting and harvesting. They were often brutalized by their masters, who were trying to squeeze as much work as possible out of them. Sugar was in great demand in Europe, and molasses made from sugar formed the basis of rum, produced in the British colonies of North America. The rum was then transported to Africa and traded for slaves that were sold in the West Indies; in turn, the sugar from islands like Hispaniola was taken to North America and became an ingredient in rum.

On the island of Hispaniola, first visited by Europeans on the voyage of Christopher Columbus in 1492, sugar as well as coffee created vast fortunes among the plantation owners. These fortunes were made on the backs of African men, women, and children. They were owned by white masters who could sell them at will, beat them mercilessly if they misbehaved, and even kill them if they resisted. In most cases, the slaves lacked the weapons and the organizing skills to rebel successfully. They were kept illiterate by their masters and strictly prevented from meeting together by Black Codes that controlled their entire lives. These laws restricted slaves from having any representation or government and made it illegal for them to learn to read or write. Nevertheless, some did try to throw off the white yoke, escaping into the mountains and swamps where they lived free. Others rose up, but they were generally defeated by the white plantation owners and the soldiers who defended the European governments that ruled the islands.

However, there was a single exception to this general rule—a successful revolt led by a man who achieved what seemed impossible. His life was a mixture of failure and success, kindness and brutality, brilliant leadership abilities and foolhardiness. In short, he was much like the other great leaders of world history, but he stands out because he was a black slave. He called himself Toussaint L'Ouverture, the man who established the free, independent island nation of Haiti.

1

The Black Spartacus

Over two thousand years ago, a slave named Spartacus led a revolt against the powerful armies of the Roman Empire. Spartacus had been captured by the Romans and was trained to be a gladiator—a man who fought to the death with a sword against his opponent in front of a huge crowd of cheering spectators. (The word "gladiator" comes from the Latin *gladius*, meaning "short sword," the weapon generally used in the arena.) In 73 BCE, Spartacus and seventy other slaves staged a revolt at Capua, the site of a gladiator training school in southern Italy. After stealing weapons from the Romans, the slaves were joined by others in the area and eventually set up their headquarters near Mount Vesuvius.

At first, the Roman Republic paid scant attention to the uprising, believing that a small force of trained, battle-hardened soldiers would put a quick end to the revolt. But the Romans miscalculated, and in 72 BCE the government was forced to send two legions of crack troops to strike at the heart of the rebellion. At first, the legions proved their superiority, defeating a detachment of gladiators led by a former slave named Crixus. But the Roman victory proved short-lived because Spartacus avenged the loss with a bloody and decisive triumph near

During the 1790s, Toussaint L'Ouverture led the only slave revolt in world history that successfully defeated the white masters and established an independent nation, Haiti.

Herculaneum. By this time, many more slaves had joined the revolt, and the army numbered approximately seventy thousand troops. With this force, Spartacus headed north toward the Alps, where he stunned the Republic with another great victory.

As a result, the Roman Republic dispatched another larger army, led by Marcus Licinius Crassus—the wealthiest man in Rome. At first, Spartacus defeated one wing of the army that had tried to surprise his troops. But the superior forces that Rome had put in the field finally gained the upper hand in a series of hard-fought battles. Spartacus and the remains of his army were pushed southward until their backs were up against the Mediterranean Sea.

Instead of surrendering, however, Spartacus decided to fight in one last battle in 71 BCE. He almost scored an improbable victory, nearly killing Crassus during the struggle. But his troops were eventually overwhelmed and slaughtered by superior Roman forces, and Spartacus himself was killed on the battlefield.

Although Spartacus might be gone and his revolt defeated, his name was not forgotten, and it continued to be recalled over the centuries. Slavery itself did not disappear either, and other slaves dreamed of a successful rebellion against their masters. Slave revolts continued to occur but it was not until the 1790s in the Caribbean in the French colony of Saint-Domingue that another leader emerged to rival Spartacus.

Indeed, this slave became known as the Black Spartacus. As an observer in Saint-Domingue wrote during the period: "Natural liberty is the right which nature has given to everyone to dispose of himself according to his

Spartacus led a slave revolt among the gladiators of ancient Rome that has never been forgotten, but it was eventually defeated by the Romans and Spartacus was killed.

will … A courageous chief only is wanted. Where is he? He will appear, doubt it not; he will come forth and raise the sacred standard of liberty."[1]

And he did appear. His name was Toussaint L'Ouverture, and he became the only leader of a black slave revolt in history to overthrow the white masters and their colonial government and to achieve total victory.

2
Toussaint and Saint-Domingue

The first Europeans to settle on the island of Hispaniola—one of the largest in the Caribbean—were Christopher Columbus and his sailors, who arrived there in 1492. When Columbus landed, his expedition encountered the Taino Indians, who had lived on the island for many years. The Spanish tried to con-

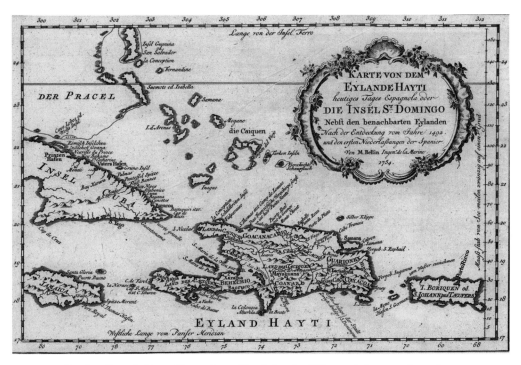

During the eighteenth century, the island of Hispaniola was shared by the Spanish colony of Santo Domingo and the French colony of Saint-Domingue, later called Haiti.

vert the tribespeople to Christianity, but eventually the white settlers simply enslaved the Indians to work on their farms and plantations. The Spanish themselves felt that manual labor was beneath them. By the early 1500s, the Indians had been almost completely wiped out either by backbreaking labor or by diseases brought to the New World by the Spanish.

To take the place of the Indians, the Spanish began to import slaves from Africa. During tribal warfare in West Africa, men, women, and even children were routinely captured and sold into slavery. The slaves were taken to the coast of Africa, where European slave traders had established forts to hold the captured slaves. After paying the African tribesmen, the slavers loaded their captives onto ships for the New World. At first Portuguese sea captains were the main slavers, but

Plate 25   pag: 54

38.

The Sugar works

The Sugar Canes

Life on a sugar plantation involved back-breaking work that took the lives of many African slaves.

gradually they were joined by British, Dutch, French, and American slave traders.

Slavers made a 10 percent to 30 percent profit for every African they brought to the New World to work on the plantations. The slave captains, known as tight packers, loaded hundreds of captives onto their ships for the journey westward. Since the white slavers regarded Africans as subhuman, the conditions were deplorable. Slaves were shackled and packed below deck into the ship's hold where the air was thick with the smell of vomit and human waste. The slaves were allowed to come on deck once a day for exercise that might keep them relatively healthy, and they were fed a meager diet—just enough to keep them alive. During a trip across the Atlantic that might take from five weeks to three months, many slaves suffered from seasickness that made the journey even worse.

"The Negroes," according to one planter, "are unjust, cruel, barbarous, half-human, treacherous, deceitful, thieves, drunkards, proud, lazy, unclean, shameless, jealous to fury, and cowards. The safety of the whites demands that we keep the Negroes in the most profound ignorance. I have reached the stage of believing firmly that one must treat the Negroes as one treats beasts."[1]

Historian Peter Kolchin, an expert on slavery in the Americas, has written: "Men were kept in chains; women and children, fewer in number, were sometimes allowed greater freedom of movement. In ships run by 'tight packers,' who deplored the waste of space provided by

TRANSPORTING SLAVES FROM AFRICA

Historian C. L. R. James wrote a groundbreaking history of the revolution in Saint-Domingue and the conditions that led up to it titled *The Black Jacobins*. Describing the tight packers, in which slaves were transported to the New World, he wrote:

The slaves were collected in the interior, fastened one to the other in columns, loaded with heavy stones of 40 to 50 pounds [18 to 23 kilograms] in weight to prevent attempts to escape, and then marched the long journey to the sea, sometimes hundreds of miles, the weak and sick dropping to die in the African jungle ... On the ships the slaves were packed in the hold on galleries one above the other. Each was given only four or five feet [1.2 or 1.5 m] in length and two or three feet [.6 or .9 m] in height so that they could neither lie at full length nor sit upright ... coming up once a day for exercise ... The close proximity of so many naked human beings, their bruised and festering flesh, the fetid air ... the accumulation of filth, turned these holds into a hell. During the storms the hatches were battened down, and in the close and loathsome darkness they hurled from one side to another by the heaving vessel, held in position by the chains on their bleeding flesh no place on earth ... concentrated so much misery as the hold of a slave ship.[2]

holds five feet [1.5 meters] in height and consequently installed middle shelves, creating two levels of two and a half feet [.8 m], slaves were often crammed together so closely they could barely move."[3]

Toussaint's Family Heritage

Toussaint L'Ouverture was the grandson of an African tribal king. Toussaint's father, Gaou-Guinou, was captured during tribal warfare in the early 1700s, taken to the coast of Africa along with other tribesmen, and transported to the Caribbean. The trip across the Atlantic was known as the Middle Passage and might take a few weeks if the weather was calm or much longer in rough and stormy seas. By the time Gaou-Guinou reached the island of Hispaniola, it had changed greatly from the days when it was first settled by Christopher Columbus and the Spanish. Spain now controlled only the eastern half the island, known as Santo Domingo. The western half of the island was a French colony, called Saint-Domingue.

Gaou-Guinou had been transported to Saint-Domingue with his wife, Affiba, and their two children. They were purchased by the Breda plantation, a lucrative land holding owned by the Breda family and located near the town of Cap Français. During the eighteenth century, Saint-Domingue became known as the "Pearl of the Antilles," that is, the West Indies. Saint-Domingue was the wealthiest French colony because of its vast sugar and coffee plantations.

According to historian C. L. R. James, during the 1760s the colony shipped over 120,000,000 pounds (54,431,084 kg) of sugar each year to Western Europe. This amounted to 40 percent of the sugar consumed on

BLACK CODE

The lives of the slaves were governed by a series of strict rules, known as the Black Code. These were created by plantation owners to prevent the slaves from beginning a rebellion that might end with violence to the owners and their family. Every slave society in the Americas had such a code, including the slave states in North America. The Black Code in Saint-Domingue included the following:

> *Article XV. We forbid slaves from carrying any offensive weapons or large sticks, at the risk of being whipped and having the weapons confiscated.*
>
> *Article XVI. We also forbid slaves who belong to different masters from gathering, either during the day or at night, under the pretext of a wedding or other excuse, either at one of the master's houses or elsewhere ... They shall risk corporal punishment.*
>
> *Article XVIII. We forbid slaves from selling sugar cane, for whatever reason or occasion, even with the permission of their master, at the risk of a whipping.*
>
> *Article XLII. The masters may also, when they believe that their slaves so deserve, chain them and have them beaten with rods or straps. They shall be forbidden however from torturing them or mutilating any limb at the risk of having the slaves confiscated and having extraordinary charges brought against them.*[4]

the European continent. In addition, the French colony's coffee plantations produced 60 percent of Europe's coffee. Most of the work on these plantations was done by slaves. There were almost 300,000 of them on the island with over forty thousand imported to Saint-Domingue each year. They were ruled by a tiny population of about thirty thousand white slave owners.[5]

Life among the slave population was especially brutal. African slaves were governed by the Code Noir, or "the Black Code." This required the slave owners to feed, house, and clothe the slaves. But the Black Code also gave them permission to work the slaves to death and punish them mercilessly if they disobeyed.

The Black Code supposedly forbad slave owners from torturing and killing their slaves. Nevertheless, a former slave recalled that this did not stop slave owners from brutally punishing any slave who did not follow orders. Some were drowned in the rivers, thrown into the water tied in sacks and weighted down with stones. Others were crucified on trees and still others, tied up, thrown into holes and covered with dirt so they smothered to death. Whippings were unusually severe. A slave who upset his master might receive one hundred blows with a whip, although the Black Code specified that only half that number was allowed.[6] Those who were not mistreated died of yellow fever or malaria—fatal illnesses carried by mosquitoes.

This vast army of slaves worked long hours each day on the plantations. On the sugar plantations, work often began at 4 a.m. and continued until midnight. Many slaves worked in the fields cutting sugar cane. Then the cane was brought by cart to a mill located on the plantation owner's estate. Inside each mill, slaves fed the sugar cane

Toussaint was among the very few slaves who learned how to read. Among the books he read was *The Prince*, by Niccolo Machiavelli, a manual written in the 1500s that taught leaders how to govern their lands successfully.

between wooden or metal rollers, which crushed the cane, squeezing out the juice. Many slaves lost their fingers or their arms feeding cane between the rollers.

From the mills, the juice flowed to the boiling and curing house, where slaves poured it into a series of heated copper basins. The syrupy sugar was thickened and eventually crystallized. Then the sugar was poured into barrels or sugar molds, shaped like cones for transportation to Europe.

Many slaves survived for only a few years under brutal overseers—slave drivers—who worked them continually. Somehow Gaou-Guinou survived and died as a very old man in 1804.

Toussaint's Early Years

Historians are uncertain of the exact year of Toussaint's birth. Records were not kept about most slaves. But his birth probably occurred somewhere between 1739 and 1746 on the Breda plantation. He was a frail, sickly child nicknamed Farras-Baton—that is, "Throwaway Stick." It was his frail health, however, that may have saved Toussaint from an early death in the cane fields or the sugar mills. Instead, he was one of the few African slaves who learned to read and write. Under the Black Code, this was prohibited. White slave owners feared that literate slaves who read about revolutionary ideas might communicate with each other by written message and band together in armed revolt. But Toussaint was fortunate because he was taught reading and writing probably by a freed African slave named Pierre Baptiste. Some slaves who were skilled as carpenters, blacksmiths, animal trainers, or other artisans were permitted by their masters to do paid work at other plantations. Although the masters collected most of this money, a few slaves managed to save enough to buy their freedom.

Toussaint wrote in French and read the work of the Roman philosopher Epictetus, as well as *The Prince*, by the Italian author Niccolo Machiavelli. In this book, Machiavelli instructed political leaders about the skills they needed to become successful. Born on the Breda plantation, the young slave was known as Toussaint at Breda. Slaves were frequently named according to the plantations on which they lived. Toussaint's job was to care for the plantation's livestock, such as pigs and horses. Toussaint showed a special talent for this type of work, especially training horses and providing animals with medical care. Eventually in 1772, when a new manager named Bayon de Libertat came to the plantation, he appointed Toussaint his coachman and his chief assistant. "Having fathomed the character of Toussaint," the manager said, "I entrusted to him the principal branch of my management, and the care of the livestock. Never was my confidence in him disappointed."[7]

In 1782, when Toussaint was in his forties, he married a woman named Suzanne Simone Baptiste. Together they raised three sons: Placide, Isaac, and Saint-Jean. Isaac, the middle son, later wrote a biography of Toussaint, from which much of his life is now known. According to his biography, Toussaint worked at two hospitals on the island of Saint-Domingue. One of these was Providence Hospital, near Cap Français, while the other was located near Haut du Cap. It was not unusual for slave owners to permit their slaves to work outside the plantations if their duties gave them time to do it. Blacks were employed as nurses and assisted doctors in surgery. From this experience, Toussaint received a broad training in medicine. He added this expertise to a growing knowledge of veterinary medicine that had begun to make him well known across the island.

About 1777, Toussaint was set free by the plantation manager Bayon de Libertat, probably because of his skills as an assistant manager on the plantation. As Toussaint later explained in 1797, "Twenty years ago the heavy burden of slavery was lifted from me by one of those men who think more of their duties to fulfill toward oppressed humanity than the product of work of an unfortunate being. Here I speak of my former master, the virtuous Bayon."[8]

After becoming free, Toussaint himself became a plantation owner at Petit Cormier, purchasing the property with money earned from his work. There he supervised thirteen slaves who grew coffee and various types of food crops that were sold to other plantations. These crops could be grown with far fewer slaves than sugar cane. In Saint-Domingue, as well as in the southern United States, there were a few free blacks who owned plantations and slaves. Toussaint became one of them.

Most of the work on the plantations was performed by slaves, many of whom were literally worked to death. So each year, the planters had to import a large group of slaves to replace those who had died.

In addition to the free blacks on Saint-Domingue, there was also a group of mulattoes. These were the children of black mothers and white fathers who had been freed by their fathers. White plantation owners regularly produced children with black slave women, who had little choice but to submit to their white masters.

These freed inhabitants of Saint-Domingue formed a separate class, below the whites, but above the 300,000 slaves on the island. In the early 1790s, Toussaint would begin to use his leadership skills and his relationships with slaves and freed blacks on the island to initiate a revolution that changed Saint-Domingue forever.

3
Big Whites and Small Whites

Society in Saint-Domingue was shaped like a giant pyramid. There were about thirty thousand white settlers at the top; about thirty-two thousand mulattoes and free blacks, like Toussaint, in the middle; and about 300,000 slaves at the bottom. At the pinnacle of the pyramid were the so-called big whites, or *grande blancs*, that included plantation owners and well-to-do merchants. Below them were the people called small whites, or *petits blancs*, who were professionals, like doctors and lawyers as well as clerks, carpenters, and store owners.

Beneath the whites, both big and small, were a number of mulattoes, or people of color who were the children of white men and black women. Many of them had been freed by their white fathers, but others were held as slaves, and they could be sold off at any time by their owners. Of course, this split up families, and the enslaved could be separated from their children and might not see them again for years. Some mulattoes became artisans, like stonemasons or carpenters. Others were freed household servants who lived in the homes of their fathers or other white planters. Although many were free, mulattoes still faced various types of discrimination from whites who looked down on them because of their skin color.

Skin color in Saint-Domingue determined a person's place in the social hierarchy; white plantation owners were at the top, black slaves at the bottom.

As historian C. L. R. James wrote, mulattoes "were forbidden to wear swords and sabers and European dress. They were forbidden to buy ammunition except by special permission with the exact quantity stated. They were forbidden to meet together … They were forbidden to play European games … they were forbidden to take the titles of Monsieur and Madame … [and] if a white man ate in their house, they could not sit at table with him."[1] Mulattoes were not considered to be citizens; nevertheless, they were required to join a special police force charged with arresting escaped slaves. Thus, the mulattoes had to cooperate with the white plantation owners, but they were not allowed the same privileges or place in society. This angered the mulattoes, especially the small number who had become well-to-do from their businesses.

The mulattoes, in their turn, looked down on the free blacks, like Toussaint, because their skin was usually darker. In fact, mulattoes also discriminated among themselves based on skin color. C. L. R. James wrote, "the man of color who was nearly white despised the man of color who was only half-white, who in turn despised the man of color who was only a quarter white, and so on through all the shades."[2]

"No small white was a servant, no white man did any work that he could get a Negro to do for him. A barber summoned to attend to a customer appeared in silk attire, hat under his arm, sword at his side, cane under his elbow, followed by four Negroes. One of them combed the hair, another dressed it, a third curled it and the fourth finished. While they worked the

Cap Français was a major port in Saint-Domingue and a primary center of white culture and wealth in the French colony.

employer presided over the various operations. At the slightest slackness, at the slightest mistake, he boxed the cheek of the unfortunate slave so hard that often he knocked him over. The slave picked himself up without any sign of resentment, and resumed." —C. L. R. James[3]

Governing the Colony

Above all the classes in Saint-Domingue was a group of about five hundred French officials who governed the colony. Among them was the governor, who was a French nobleman. The governor was assisted by the intendant, who was in charge of the finances needed to maintain the colony as well as the courts of justice. In each district of the colony, there was a military commandant and other officials, who were backed up by regiments of soldiers from France.

Most of the colony was quite rural, dotted by large plantations, especially along the fertile North Plain. Here Cap Français was the chief port. Slave ships landed here as well as ships bearing goods from France and those sailing to

France with products from the colony. The other major city was the capital, Port-au-Prince.

Saint-Domingue, like other colonies controlled by France and other colonial nations, like Great Britain, operated under the mercantile system. A similar system controlled the economic relations between the American colonies and Britain. The laws of this system required that a colony buy the products it needed only from the colonial ruling nation, like France. In addition, the colony could only sell its own goods to that nation. This meant that a colony and its ruling nation would depend on one another for trade and, thus, for a healthy economy.

The mercantile system in the French empire was known as "the exclusive"—that is, the colony had to trade exclusively with France. In practice, this meant that Saint-Domingue had to purchase all its slaves from French slavers. By the late eighteenth century tens of thousands of slaves were being shipped to the island annually. There was a constant need for more slaves because many died from disease, like malaria and yellow fever, or they were worked to death by their owners. This enabled the slave traders in French coastal cities like Nantes and Marseilles to grow rich. In addition, the islanders were required to buy European goods such as wine, furniture, paper, carpets, and fine clothing from France.

In return, the French merchants had a monopoly on the products grown on the island and could set any price they wanted to pay for them. By the last half of the 1700s, Saint-Domingue was shipping 72,000,000 pounds (32,658,651 kg) of raw sugar, 51,000,000 pounds (23,133,211 kg) of white sugar, two million pounds (907,185 kg) of cotton, and

OBSERVATIONS OF A VISITOR

Justin Girod-Chantrans was a Swiss traveler who visited Saint-Domingue and wrote about his journey in the 1780s. He recalled his visit to a plantation on the island, where:

"[There] were about a hundred men and women of different ages, all occupied in digging ditches in a cane-field, the majority of them naked or covered with rags. The sun shone down with full force on their heads. Sweat rolled from all parts of their bodies. Their limbs, weighed down by the heat, fatigued with the weight of their picks and by the resistance of the clay soil baked hard enough to break their implements ... The pitiless eye of the Manager patrolled the gang and several foremen [slave drivers] armed with long whips moved periodically between them, giving stinging blows to all who, worn out by fatigue, were compelled to take a rest—men or women, young or old."4

one million pounds (453,592 kg) of indigo to France each year.[5]

The colonists on Saint-Domingue knew that their plantations were making the French rich. And many of the plantation owners greatly resented having to operate under the exclusive system when they might have made more money trading with other colonial empires such as the Spanish or the British. Gradually this resentment would grow until it finally boiled over.

A SONG OF SLAVES

Resentment among the slaves on the plantations was quite common because of the way they were treated by their masters. Most slaves did not submit willingly but held the seeds of rebellion in their hearts. A few escaped from the plantations into the mountains. Others showed their resentment by refusing to work and many slaves on the plantation regularly sang a song of defiance that their white owners could not understand:

Eh! Eh! Bomba! Heu! Heu!
Canga, bafio te!
Canga, moune de le!
Canga, do ki la!
Canga, li!

This meant: "We swear to destroy the whites and all that they possess; let us die rather than fail to keep this vow."[6] Other songs that the slaves sung were about their faith or about how they survived despite the inhumanity of slavery. Many of these songs were passed on for generations.

Resentment Among the Slaves

Meanwhile, resentment had been growing over the years among the slaves who were continually mistreated by their owners. According to one history written in this period, the whites regarded the slaves as "cruel, barbarous, half-human, treacherous, deceitful, thieves, drunkards, proud, lazy, unclean, shameless, jealous to fury, and cowards." Thus the whites saw nothing wrong in treating them like animals. As this writer added, "The safety of the whites demands that we keep the Negroes in the most profound ignorance. I have reached the stage of believing firmly that one must treat the Negroes as one treats beasts."[7]

With so many new slaves coming into the island from Africa each year, a majority had not become accustomed to life on the island and to living in bondage. Among these slaves, resentment was especially strong. It might take only a single incident—a single match—to ignite the powder necessary to start a revolution. And that match was about to be struck.

4

Winds of Change

In 1788, France faced a serious financial crisis. The government was on the verge of bankruptcy, having spent huge sums of money helping America achieve its independence and battling other nations such as Spain and Great Britain for colonial empires around the world. King Louis XVI decided that for the first time in 150 years he would call together the French legislature, known as the Estates-General, to help his government find a solution to the crisis.

Representatives of three estates met in the French assembly: the First Estate, which was made up of France's nobility; the Second Estate, which was made up of the French clergy; and the Third Estate, which was comprised of French merchants, professional people, and the vast French peasantry. One of the problems with finding a solution to the financial crisis was that the first two estates did not pay any taxes. The entire tax burden fell on the third estate. And, since each estate's representatives in the assembly voted as a unit, the First and Second Estate were likely to vote together against the Third Estate to keep the tax situation as it had been for many years.

The meeting of the Estates-General, however, acted as a signal to the wealthy planters of Saint-Domingue that the time for change might have finally arrived. For decades,

In 1789, an angry French mob stormed the French prison at the Bastille in Paris, signaling the start of a revolution that would change France and Saint-Domingue.

they had opposed the mercantile trading restrictions under the exclusive system. Now they decided to demand that they should be able to send representatives to vote in the Estates-General, which might change economic conditions across France and its empire. However, the big whites were not united in this demand. Many were aware that the calling of the Estates-General not only might lead to a larger voice in the government for the Third Estate but also might shine the light on social conditions in Saint-Domingue, where free blacks and mulattoes had few rights and the slaves had none at all.

JULIEN RAIMOND, AND VINCENT OGÉ

Born in Martinique in 1744, Julien Raimond was the son of a white French father and a mulatto mother. His mother had been born in Saint-Domingue to a planter, and Raimond grew up on the island. By the 1780s, he was a successful plantation owner with at least one hundred slaves. In the 1780s, he moved to France and became an absentee owner, like many others with plantations in Saint-Domingue.

There he worked with Vincent Ogé, a free black, who had been born in Saint-Domingue around 1750. Together they pleaded for the National Assembly to grant equal rights to free men. In 1790, the assembly voted to leave this decision up to the leaders of the colony. Raimond remained in Paris where he published articles calling for the gradual freeing of slaves. But Ogé returned to Saint-Domingue.

There he met strong opposition from the big whites who were strongly against the granting of equal rights to free blacks on the island. So Ogé began a revolution late in 1790 designed to change the political situation. However, he was no match for the French soldiers and the big whites who defeated his small army. Ogé was captured, brutally tortured, and beheaded early in 1791. The National Assembly was outraged by his execution and granted the rights of citizenship to all men of color (mulattoes) who had been born to free parents.

The Estates-General met at Versailles, the vast palace that was home to the French king as well as many of the aristocrats. The Third Estate demanded that the entire legislature should vote, not in three units but as individual representatives. Since the number of legislators in the Third Estate outnumbered those in the other two estates, they could push economic changes through the legislature.

The nobility and the clergy refused, so the Third Estate began meeting as a separate body known as the National Assembly. Meanwhile a few liberal members of the aristocracy joined the Third Estate and sat in the National Assembly. Some, like Count Honoré Mirabeau, even called for the abolition of slavery throughout the French colonial empire. In Saint-Domingue, the big whites became even more concerned that their lifestyle and their economic prosperity might be threatened if the National Assembly went too far with its reforms.

While the king opposed the actions of the National Assembly, he did little to stop it. Meanwhile, across France a severe famine and economic recession had severely affected most of the peasants, who were short of food and money. Many left the countryside and poured into towns and cities, especially the French capital, Paris. Parisians began to fear for their safety and demanded arms from the French soldiers stationed in the city to defend themselves. When the soldiers refused, a mob stormed the Bastille, a military prison and arsenal, on July 14, 1789, killing its defenders, releasing its prisoners, and causing fear to spread across France.

The French celebrate Bastille Day, as it is called, on July 14 each year as their Independence Day.

The demands of the French Revolution were contained in the Declaration of the Rights of Man—a document that also made a profound impact on the slaves and mulattoes of Saint-Domingue.

The Revolution Gathers Force

In August 1789, the National Assembly passed the Declaration of the Rights of Man. It stated, "Men are born and remain free and equal in rights." These natural rights included "liberty, property, security, and resistance to oppression." Finally, King Louis XVI decided that the National Assembly had gone too far and tried to disband them. Instead, they swore an oath never to adjourn. They were joined by Louis Marthe de Gouy d'Arsy, a spokesman for Saint-Domingue's big whites in France who asked for eighteen seats in the National Assembly. He said that the big whites were entitled to this number because of the population of the colony.

But Count Mirabeau rose from his seat and loudly spoke out against d'Arsy and the other planters. He said, "You claim representation proportionate to the number of the inhabitants. The free blacks are proprietors and tax-payers, and yet they have not been allowed to vote [in Saint-Domingue]. And as for the slaves, either they are men or they are not; if the colonists consider them to be men, let them free them and make them electors and eligible for seats."[1]

The important issues of slavery and freedom were now being discussed in France—and news of the Bastille and the debates in the National Assembly soon reached Saint-Domingue. Meanwhile a delegation of free blacks was calling on the French to grant them representation in the assembly. They were led by Julien Raimond, a free black and a landowner in Saint-Domingue who had sailed to Paris in the 1780s to plead the cause of free blacks and ask that they be given the rights of citizens. But the big whites refused to listen.

Vincent Ogé led a revolution in Saint-Domingue, demanding more rights for mulattoes.

Meanwhile, in Saint-Domingue, white leaders established the Colonial Assembly in the city of Saint-Marc, along the coast. After some debate, a majority of the delegates voted to create a constitution giving them control of the government of the island. In France, the National Assembly opposed this action, believing that it was a call for independence. The royal governor was ordered to shut down the Colonial Assembly and abolish the constitution. He succeeded with the help of some of the big whites who had been opposed to the assembly's actions.

But this did not end the calls for reform. Large groups of free blacks began calling for more rights. And Ogé, before his execution, had even threatened to free the slaves so they could help his uprising. These events frightened the big whites, who began to see that their future on the island might be threatened. They also opposed the decision by the French National Assembly in 1791 to grant the rights of citizenship to all men of color whose parents had been free.

In fact, this decision by the National Assembly had so inflamed the whites on the island that they launched a revolution against the French government in Saint-Domingue, which the governor was unable to control. The white population also persuaded the National Assembly in Paris to revoke its decision to provide equal rights to free men of color.

But it was too late to save the situation in Saint-Domingue. By successfully revolting against the government, the whites had signaled to the other groups in Saint-Domingue that a revolution might be possible. Once the whites had opened the door, they could never close it again. And they would be overrun by a slave revolt that changed the island forever.

45

5
Slave Revolt in Saint-Domingue

Slave revolts were not new in the Caribbean islands or in North America. In 1733, a slave revolt erupted on the Dutch island of St. John in the West Indies. The Danish settlers built sugar, indigo, and cotton plantations that were worked by black slaves. There were over one hundred plantations by the 1730s and more than one thousand slaves. The white population was comprised of only about two hundred settlers. Some slaves had already escaped from the plantations to live as Maroons—groups of free blacks who lived in the woods and jungles on the island. They wanted to avoid the severe punishments that whites imposed on them under the Slave Code of 1733. Similar to the Black Code on Saint-Domingue, it permitted slave owners to whip their slaves or even amputate arms or legs for various offenses.

On St. John, many of the slaves were from the Akwamu tribe. They had once been very powerful warriors in West Africa. But the tribe was eventually defeated in battle and many of their warriors sold into slavery. Early in 1733 on St. John, some of these slaves began meeting with their leaders, known as King June and King Bolombo, to plan a revolt. In November, a rebellion broke out at the plantation of Johannes Sodtmann, who lived in Coral Bay. The slaves took over the Danish fort at the

When a slave rebellion broke out in Saint-Domingue in 1791, Toussaint was not among its early leaders. But he eventually joined the revolt and soon distinguished himself for his leadership skills.

harbor, while others attacked nearby plantations, killing many of the white families who lived on them. In a short time, the former slaves controlled most of the island.

But some white plantation owners successfully drove off the attacks. The Danes finally got messages through to the French island of Martinique, asking for help. Traveling more than 300 miles (483 kilometers), French ships finally arrived, carrying troops who put down the revolt by the end of August 1734.

A few years earlier, a Maroon war had broken out on the British island of Jamaica. Although British troops fought back, they were never able to defeat the Maroons. Under the leadership of a black man named Cudjoe, they battled the British to a standstill. Eventually, in 1739, the government signed a truce with the Maroons who retained their freedom in return for promising to help the British drive off any foreign attack and participate in the capture of any escaped slaves.

In 1760, this agreement became essential to the defeat of a slave rebellion on Jamaica. It was led by Tacky, a former African chief who had been sold into slavery. The slaves escaped from their plantations and attacked a nearby store, killing the owner and stealing muskets and ammunition. Some of Tacky's lieutenants where religious leaders who claimed they could not be killed by musket fire. When the British succeeded in killing some of them, the rebellion among the other slaves began to fizzle. Tacky led them into the Jamaican hills, but they were followed by the Maroons who knew the terrain very well. Eventually one of them killed Tacky, and the rest of the former slaves, who were holed up in a cave, killed themselves.

The slave revolt in Saint-Domingue would begin in much the same way and for much the same reasons—a desire among the slaves to escape the control of white plantation owners and win their freedom. But gradually the aims of the revolt changed, becoming a struggle for a free, independent country that would be called Haiti.

Rebellion Erupts in the North Province

On Sunday, August 14, 1791, a large gathering of slaves from plantations in the north province of Saint-Domingue—where Cap Français was located—met in a great voodoo ceremony. The ceremony may have been held in the woods of Bois Caiman or on the plantation of Lenormand de Mezy. Most slaves in Saint-Domingue believed in voodoo, spiced with a dash of Christianity. According to voodoo beliefs, the souls of the dead hovered around the earth ready to return and inhabit the bodies of the living. When this happened, the living were infused with great passion and energy from the souls of the dead to carry out their mission on earth—whatever this mission might be.

Leading the ceremony was Boukman Dutty, a large man who was a voodoo high priest. He and other leaders of the slaves worked as slave drivers, or people who oversaw slaves on the plantations. Dutty and others were skilled at leading slaves because of their experience doing this on the plantations. Among the other slave drivers at the ceremony was Jean-François Papillon, a Maroon, as well as Georges Biassou and Jeannot Billet. Billet was one of the most brutal rebel leaders—a man who thought nothing of torturing and murdering his prisoners.

According to one historian, Dutty told his followers at the ceremony, "Listen to the liberty which speaks in the hearts of all of us."[1] And the slaves did listen. Eight days

After years of brutal treatment at the hands of the whites, slaves rose up in 1791, killing many white plantation owners and their families.

later they rose up on the northern plain and overran the rich plantations of the white colonists. The sugar cane and coffee plants were burned creating a huge, dark cloud that surrounded the entire area. The slaves also attacked the homes of the whites, killing hundreds of men, women, and children. As the insurrection continued, thousands of slaves joined the revolt. Many of the whites ran for Cap Français, which was heavily defended by the French soldiers.

Toussaint had not participated in the first uprisings. He remained at Breda, where he tried to keep things as calm as possible. He urged the more than three hundred slaves who lived on the plantation to keep working so they could bring in a large harvest of sugar cane. Toussaint also protected Madame de Libertat, the wife of the owner. Her husband was away at another of his plantations. When he returned, Bayon de Libertat later wrote that some of his fields had been set ablaze but that Toussaint and the slave driver, Bruno, had successfully stopped the fires.

SAVED BY SLAVES

Some owners who were caught by the slaves were spared. One of the plantation owners recalled hearing his dog bark in the middle of the night, followed by the sounds of men outside his house. He said, "I jumped out of my bed and shouted, 'Who goes there?' A voice like thunder answered me: 'It is death!'" Fortunately, this man was saved by Boukman Dutty, who had worked on the plantation and liked him. Another woman said later that she had been protected by her own slaves who led her into hiding in one of their small homes. They protected her there while rampaging rebels overran her plantation.[2]

Eventually Toussaint led Madame de Libertat away toward Cap Français and safety. Afterward, he left Breda and joined the rebellion led by Biassou. Toussaint, with his knowledge of medicine, became known as *médecin général*, general doctor, and this title appears on his letters written during this early period of the rebellion.

"When I arrived the next evening," Bayon de Libertat recalled, "all the scorched cane had been cut and pressed, and they were just finishing cooking the sugar which had been extracted from it. Toussaint came before me with a pained expression and said, 'We have had an accident, but don't

alarm yourself, the loss is not serious; I wanted to spare you the sight of it when you arrived, but you have come too soon.' Toussaint displayed an inexpressible joy to see me constantly in the midst of the blacks, giving them my orders to arouse their vigilance and their courage—and this at a time when it was enough to be white to be massacred."[3]

The Rebellion Grows

While the French held Cap Français, the slaves controlled the countryside, and the rebellion in the northern province reached a stalemate. Any French forces that ventured out from the city, hoping to defeat slave armies, were often surprised by their highly effective tactics. As one soldier said, "[The slaves] formed groups hiding in thickets before falling on their enemy. They even withdrew swiftly into the undergrowth. We are dealing with an enemy, who instead of making a concerted attack … was disposed in small groups so that they were able to surround or wipe out isolated or small detachments. It was a new type of warfare, more dangerous because it was unknown."[4] First the French heard the sound of a large conch shell being blown from the woods, then the fire of muskets, and finally they found themselves overwhelmed by the attack of the black soldiers.

The blacks had known and used a similar type of guerrilla warfare in Africa. But in Europe, where armies formed up in long lines and fought each other on open battlefields with guns and bayonets, it was unknown. However, even these successful guerrilla tactics did

During the early months of the slave rebellion, large plantations around Cap Français were burned and their owners murdered by the slave armies.

not prevent some of the slaves from being killed. An estimated four thousand died in the opening months of the rebellion. Then, in November 1791, Boukman Dutty died in a battle with French soldiers, causing great alarm among many of his followers who had depended on him to lead them into freedom.

Meanwhile another rebellion had broken out in the west province, near the capital, Port-au-Prince. The freemen of color—mulattoes—had risen up to demand the same rights as the whites in the colony. Led by André Rigaud, a mulatto slave owner, they met in a local Catholic church and resolved to rebel rather than wait for the white colonial legislature to give them their rights. They were joined by some of the white plantation owners who believed that through joint action they could protect their interests against the type of rebellion that had broken out in the north. And these whites agreed that freemen of color should have all the rights of white citizens on the island.

The freemen also hired some former black slaves to fight for them, and with this force, they succeeded in capturing Port-au-Prince near the end of October 1791.

Toussaint and the Rebellion

The slave revolt in Saint-Domingue frightened other colonial governments across the Caribbean. The British government that ruled Jamaica feared that their plantation owners might be attacked, repeating the Maroon War of the 1730s. In the United States, southern plantation owners also feared that their slaves might revolt and destroy the plantations. A revolt in South Carolina in the 1730s had been put down but not before more than twenty whites had been killed. In 1791, a slave rebellion also began in Louisiana—a colony of the Spanish—although it was unsuccessful.

Meanwhile, the Spanish in Santo Domingo had become involved in the revolt inside the French colony. They wanted to undermine the colony of Saint-Domingue and take control of the lucrative sugar plantations. So the Spanish governor sent arms to the slaves who had risen up in Saint-Domingue, hoping that this might tip the balance of power against the French plantation owners.

By the end of 1791, Toussaint had become one of the leaders of the rebellion. Historians are not certain how this had happened. But they do know that he had achieved a reputation for himself as a leader and skilled doctor. Many black troops looked up to him, and other leaders of the slave revolt seemed to trust his judgment.

At first, Toussaint's aim, as well as those of the other leaders, was not freedom for all the slaves. They simply wanted to stop some of the abuses under the Black Code.

These included harsh punishments like whipping, as well as forbidding the slaves to take days off to plant their own crops. In return, Toussaint asked for complete freedom for a few of the black leaders and offered to return all the white hostages captured during the rebellion.

But the Colonial Assembly made up of whites in Cap Français refused. Biassou was very upset when he heard of their decision and threatened to murder the white prisoners that he had captured. But Toussaint protected them. As one hostage later said, "braving all dangers, he tried to save us, were himself to be the victim of the monster's (Biassou's) rage."[5] Early in 1792, Toussaint, at the head of 150 cavalrymen, eventually led the prisoners to safety inside the walls of Cap Français. In return, Toussaint hoped to meet with the Colonial Assembly and negotiate a peace treaty.

But the whites refused. At this point, historians believe that Toussaint realized that the only thing that would change the situation was to lead all the slaves to freedom and overthrow white rule in the colony. This now became his mission and the goal of the rebellion.

6

1793–1794

Early in 1793, the French government executed King Louis XVI. What had begun a few years earlier as a small revolution designed to make the laws of France fairer and more liberal had become increasingly radical. The king and many members of the nobility had been rounded up and executed. And a year after the king's death, his wife, Queen Marie Antoinette, would also be executed on the guillotine. As France became more radical, the situation in Saint-Domingue changed, too.

France was no longer a monarchy ruled by a king and an aristocracy. It was now a republic governed by a national legislature and an executive made up of radical reformers. The republic sent a civil commission to Saint-Domingue, and its three commissioners were charged with making sure that the island's government became more like the one in France. One of the commissioners, Léger-Félicité Sonthonax, had no use for the plantation owners who dominated the island. He wanted to ensure that the Maroons had the same rights as the big whites, much as France itself was ensuring that all citizens were equal.

In 1793, the French army led by General Laveaux battled the black army led by Toussaint for control of the colony of Saint-Domingue.

Under the direction of the new commission, French military leader Étienne Laveaux began to retake territory that had fallen to the former slaves the previous year. However, Laveaux's success turned out to be short-lived. Toussaint and other black leaders were receiving arms from the Spanish and, along with their troops, soon decided to join the Spanish army. Toussaint believed that, at least for the time being, this might be the best way to defeat the French. He had no illusions that Spain really wanted to free the slaves. They needed slaves to run the plantations after the French were driven out and the Spanish took over. But Toussaint also knew that the new French Republic was unprepared to give the slaves their freedom. Sonthonax feared that freeing the slaves would "undoubtedly lead to the massacre of all the whites."[1]

> **The Spanish controlled one part of the island of Hispaniola, so it was an easy task for them to help the slave revolt. Toussaint was grateful for Spanish support and proved to be a loyal soldier in the Spanish army. "If God were to descend to earth," wrote Toussaint's Spanish superior, the Marquis d'Hermona, "he could inhabit no purer heart than that of Toussaint L'Ouverture."[2]**

The situation in Saint-Domingue had become politically very complicated. Toussaint and the former slaves now fought alongside the Spanish. The French government on the island, led by Sonthonax and many of the big whites, was trying to recapture the colony and defeat the former slaves. Sonthonax was also an ally of the mulattoes. Meanwhile, the small whites opposed equal rights for the mulattoes, whom they disliked as much as they did the big whites. The small whites had captured Port-au-Prince a year earlier and established this city as their main headquarters. In April 1793, Sonthonax led a land and sea attack on the port, trapping the small whites inside. A short time later, they surrendered.

While Sonthonax had retaken a large part of the territory lost during the civil wars, the former black slaves had not put down their arms. The commissioners feared that the blacks' alliance with Spain might achieve a victory that would lead to a completely new government dominated by Toussaint and other black leaders. They also feared that such a victory might jeopardize the wealth of the island and its importance to the economy of France. Therefore the commissioners declared that all the slaves in Saint-Domingue should be freed. They did not actually support freedom but feared that unless they agreed to this step, the future of Saint-Domingue might be completely out of their control.

But even this was not enough. The leaders of the free slaves, including Toussaint, did not believe that the French Republic intended to let the slaves retain their freedom once the civil war had ended. In June, ten thousand of them stormed the French citadel at Cap Français, overcame the opposition of the big whites who were defending it, and burned the city. Although Sonthonax eventually arrived with his soldiers, all they found was a city that had been completely destroyed.

Toussaint's Victories

Meanwhile, during summer 1793, the black armies, led by Toussaint, had begun retaking the territory captured months earlier by Laveaux. Toussaint had already captured one of the French generals, and his success persuaded many freed slaves to join his army. Nevertheless, the war against the French had become even more complicated because there was no unity among the black leaders. They began to disagree among themselves, and their followers began shooting at each other. Meanwhile, the Spanish had also revealed that they had no intention of freeing the slaves once Spain took over the colony. Spain had begun to ally itself with the French plantation owners, the big whites, whom they needed to safeguard the plantations so they could continue producing coffee and sugar.

Since the black leaders were no longer united with all of those who fought for Spain, the Spanish invasion had begun to weaken. With the gradual defeat of Spain, it looked like the French Republic might be able to regain control of the colony. There was also a chance, although not guaranteed, that slavery might permanently end in Saint-Domingue—as the commission had announced in 1793.

L'OUVERTURE

How did Toussaint Breda become Toussaint L'Ouverture? Historians are not quite sure. Perhaps it was because of the gap or opening—in French, *ouverture*—in his front teeth. But a far more likely explanation arose from his skills as a military leader. Toussaint had read about great military leaders of the past, such as the Roman general Julius Caesar. And Toussaint's ability to bounce back and continually outwit all the other military leaders on Saint-Domingue became legendary during this

Toussaint learned to be a general by studying the writings of
Julius Caesar, one of the great military leaders of world history.

period. Indeed, one of the new commissioners from
France, Étienne Polverel, may have said, "What! This
man makes an Opening everywhere." [3] The word
"opening" or *ouverture* may account for the name
that Toussaint began using while he led his armies
to victory.

A British Surprise

At this moment, the war in Saint-Domingue took a new and surprising turn. Great Britain had allied itself with Spain and both were at war with France. The British regarded the French Revolution, the execution of King Louis XVI, and the beheading of Marie Antoinette as a threat to the stability of Europe. All of the major nations were ruled by kings and aristocrats. In addition, the British were interested in seizing the rich colony of Saint-Domingue for themselves. Therefore, in September 1793, a British military force landed on the island, where they immediately won the support of French plantation owners who had supported the king and the French monarchy.

The British won a series of battles against black leaders and eventually controlled one-third of the colony. Then they encountered an enemy that their generals could not defeat: disease. The island was the home of vast swarms of mosquitoes that carried two deadly diseases: malaria and yellow fever. Many of the British soldiers died of these illnesses, because unlike the island residents, they had no immunity to them. As the British died in vast numbers, their army grew weaker and weaker.

Nevertheless, the British had already begun a siege of Port-au-Prince, trapping the French commissioners and their army inside. And they had successfully stopped General Laveaux's efforts to occupy the countryside near the city. Meanwhile, the commissioners had done very little to follow through on their announcement to grant freedom for all the former slaves on the island. In May 1794, the British took control of Port-au-Prince after

In the years following the outbreak of rebellion, a British army invaded Saint-Domingue to capture the colony from France and take over the rich sugar plantations.

a long bombardment by their ships and an assault by their troops, driving out Sonthonax and the French army.

But during the summer and fall of 1794, the tide of the battle began to turn. Good news had arrived from Toussaint who had driven back the Spanish, finishing off their attempt to control the French colony. Toussaint had also defeated Jean-François Papillon and his black troops, who had been supporting the Spanish. As Toussaint reported to the French, "That operation completed, I

WHICH SIDE WAS TOUSSAINT FIGHTING FOR?

Historians have debated this question for many years. One historian, Philippe Girard, believes that Toussaint was fighting in part for himself. Girard points out that Toussaint's father had been a prince in Africa. Toussaint wanted to recapture the high social position that his father and their family had enjoyed. Girard further argues that Toussaint also wanted to acquire plantations and significant wealth. But this seems to overlook all the efforts that Toussaint was making to benefit the black slaves in the colony. This led him to support the Spanish and then the French during the revolution. While the French believed that Toussaint was fighting for them, the reality of the situation was really quite different. He had fought side by side with the French only to defeat the Spanish. But more than a year earlier, he had proclaimed that his goal was to free the slaves and bring them equality in Saint-Domingue. "I am Toussaint L'Ouverture; perhaps my name has made itself known to you," he had announced. "I have undertaken vengeance. I want Liberty and Equality to reign in Saint-Domingue. I am working to make that happen. Unite yourselves to us, brothers, and fight with us for the same cause."[4]

razed the … towns, so that the enemy could not make any attempt on them and so he will keep his distance from us. With the sabers of my cavalry I slew about ninety Spaniards—all those who in the end didn't want to surrender."[5] The French were elated, and General Laveaux sent Toussaint a red plume to wear in his hat—signifying the flag of France, which was red, white, and blue. Toussaint wore the red plume above the white plumes he had worn in the past.

7

Slaves No More

I n 1794, France became the first European empire to abolish slavery. This meant that the approximately 300,000 former slaves living in Saint-Domingue would never again belong to any master. However, as Toussaint realized, declaring an end to slavery and actually safeguarding it were two entirely different things. To preserve freedom, he and his followers must fight.

With his army of approximately four thousand troops, Toussaint had seized control of a strategic line of forts that connected the all-important north province with the western part of the island. This enabled him to move against the British in the west or the Spanish in other parts of the island. Toussaint's decision to occupy this strategic position indicates his superior generalship and his profound understanding of military strategy.

But there was more to his expert generalship. As historian Jeremy Popkin has written, "To improve his soldiers' skills, he employed captured white prisoners with military experience as trainers. No skirmish was too small to escape his attention, and he was skilled at deducing his enemies' intentions even from seemingly minor moves on their part; in addition … he had recruited a network of informants among the blacks serving the British and the Spanish."[1]

General Toussaint L'Ouverture worked with other leaders of the revolution to rid the colony of the French and preserve freedom for the former slaves.

After his decision to work with the French Republic, Toussaint announced in 1795, "We are republicans, and consequently free according to natural right. It can only be kings who dare to claim the right to reduce to slavery men like themselves, whom nature has made free."[2] But Toussaint also realized that the new government on Saint-Domingue needed a strong economic base to support itself. Therefore, he urged the freed slaves to return to the plantations to work as paid employees, planting and harvesting the sugar and coffee crops. He did not support their taking over the land themselves.

While the British had occupied part of the colony, Toussaint worked together with André Rigaud—a mulatto land owner who led the revolt in the south. Together, they won important military victories against the British who were still losing many of their soldiers to malaria and yellow fever. In fact, the British were forced to grant freedom to some of the black slaves who joined their armies—replacing the soldiers who had died.

Meanwhile, in 1795, Spain had decided to sign a peace treaty with the French Republic, ending their war. At the same time, the black leaders who had fought alongside the Spanish withdrew from the French colony once the Spanish gave up their attempt to control it. As a result, Toussaint became the primary black leader in Saint-Domingue. He had also begun receiving muskets and other supplies from the French who recognized that he alone could help safeguard the colony from foreign powers.

Toussaint's position was strengthened when Jean-Louis Villette, a mulatto general, led a revolt against the French. He captured Cap Français and arrested

General Laveaux—who had become the governor of Saint-Domingue—along with his supporters, throwing them into prison. To support his old friend Laveaux, Toussaint led an army against Villette, driving him out of the city and restoring Laveaux to power. As a reward for his help, Laveaux appointed Toussaint deputy governor of the colony.

The Fortunes of the New Government

In May 1796, the French government appointed a new civil commission for Saint-Domingue, as a signal of their support for the political situation on the island. The head of the new commission was Léger-Félicité Sonthonax. The Frenchman was a hero to many people in the colony, especially the blacks, because of his support for abolition. He was also married to a mulatto woman born on the island, Marie Eugenie Bleigeat.

Almost immediately, Sonthonax and Toussaint had to deal with a renewed attempt by the British to take control of the colony. An additional twelve thousand British troops had arrived in Saint-Domingue, strengthening their forces. But the British were incapable of destroying Toussaint's army, and by the spring of 1798 he had won a series of battles against them. The English had lost territory in the south and in the area around Port-au-Prince. Finally British commander General Thomas Maitland agreed to give up Port-au-Prince and leave the western part of the island. Later that year, the British also evacuated their remaining forts. In return, Toussaint agreed to safeguard the plantations of the white planters who had fought alongside the British. He also

In addition to sugar, coffee was also grown in the colony of Saint-Domingue and became a major export of the colony.

agreed not to carry the Saint-Domingue revolution to another colony, especially British Jamaica, which relied on slaves to work its plantations.

While Toussaint was happy to see the British depart, he also wanted to ensure the future for all the former slaves in Saint-Domingue. As Jeremy Popkin has explained, Toussaint recognized that the only way to accomplish this goal was "to have a black man like himself in charge of Saint-Domingue."[3] In 1797, he finally convinced Laveaux to return to France, arguing that the colony needed a man like Laveaux to ensure that the French government did not change its mind about abolition. The republican government had become more conservative, and Toussaint feared the possibility that it might reverse its policy. Many former planters, driven out of Saint-Domingue, had fled to France where they lobbied the government to restore the old plantation system.

Toussaint also convinced Sonthonax to return to France, arguing that he, too, was needed to defend the new political system in the colony. Meanwhile, Toussaint wrote to the new French government that "it was the blacks who, when France was threatened with losing the colony, used their arms and their weapons to conserve it."[4] With Sonthonax and Laveaux back in France, Toussaint was now the acknowledged leader of the colony.

Society in Saint-Domingue had undergone enormous changes since the slave revolt had begun six years earlier. Having achieved the same rights as other citizens, blacks could no longer be whipped or tortured by their employers on the plantations. They were free to marry and begin families without the permission of white masters, which had been the rule under the old plantation system.

Nevertheless, the people on the island still struggled. Saint-Domingue had to import much of its food from abroad because the climate was not suitable to growing many food items. Blacks were prevented from carving up the former plantations into small farms because the French government wanted to keep them intact so they could continue producing sugar and coffee. As a result, many blacks left the northern province and settled in the mountains. Here they attempted to create small

CAP FRANÇAIS

Much of Cap Français had been restored by 1797 after being burned earlier in the war. Approximately 50 percent of the burned buildings had been rebuilt. The names were changed on government buildings and town squares to reflect the fact that Toussaint and his black followers were now in charge of the colony. Some of these new names were "Liberty" and "Equality." One contemporary observer wrote, "I saw citizens of all colors doing business as tinsmiths, smelters, ironworkers, barrel-makers, shoemakers, carpenters, wagon makers, storekeepers, and so on. I saw thirty to a hundred mules loaded with coffee arriving every day during the harvest, and wagonloads of sugar." He added that former slaves had also gone back to work on the plantation: "They showed me their love of liberty went along with a love of work."[5]

farms for themselves. Others, who had joined the army during the rebellion, remained in military service instead of returning to the plantations. So coffee and sugar production declined.

There were few opportunities for blacks to improve their lives and find jobs outside the plantations or the armed forces. The French had never wanted black slaves to receive an education. So there were no schools or libraries on the island to help educate them. In addition, no white teacher had come to Saint-Domingue to change this situation. Nevertheless, the colony under Toussaint's leadership was struggling to rebuild itself.

8
Toussaint in Power

"Learn, citizens, to appreciate the glory of your new political status. In acquiring the rights that the Constitution accords to all Frenchmen, do not forget the duties it imposes on you. Be but virtuous and you will be Frenchmen and good citizens ... Work together for the prosperity of San Domingo by the restoration of agriculture, which alone can support a state and assure public well-being ... The age of fanaticism is over. The reign of law has succeeded to that of anarchy."[1]

By 1798, Toussaint was now the leader of Saint-Domingue. He might have declared the French colony an independent nation. But Toussaint realized that he needed the help of the world's major powers for his people to survive and prosper. In March, when a new French agent, General Joseph Hédouville, landed in Saint-Domingue, Toussaint welcomed him. But this did not mean that he planned to permit French power to rule the island.

When Toussaint took control of Port-au-Prince, after the British had left the island, he treated the white

Toussaint considered himself a religious man, believing in the Christian doctrines of the Catholic Church as well as in voodoo, the native religion of Hispaniola.

planters—supporters of Britain—who remained behind with open arms. Toussaint realized that he needed the big whites to run the plantations, which held the key to Saint-Domingue's future prosperity. The French Republic did not agree with this decision because many of the planters were supporters of the old French monarchy. But Toussaint was far more interested in the future of his country than he was in the opinions of the French government. However, he and Hédouville agreed that the former slaves should go back to work for the plantation owners as free, paid workers.

> **"Work together for the prosperity of Saint-Domingue by the restoration of agriculture, which alone can support a state and assure public well-being," Toussaint told his people.[2]**

Nevertheless, Hédouville believed in asserting French authority on the island. He wanted to replace Toussaint's government officials—many of them army officers—with French civil servants. But Toussaint refused. Hédouville also did not want Toussaint to have any contact with the British, who were at war with France. But Toussaint refused this request, too, because he realized that Britain had the world's most powerful navy. British ships controlled the Caribbean waters, and they were essential to supplying Toussaint's government with arms and supplies. These were desperately needed to defend the island.

Hédouville was strongly opposed to Toussaint's willingness to deal with supporters of the French monarchy; nevertheless, many of them served as secretaries to his government officials. They could not read or write, since they were former slaves. Referring to his alliance with the monarchists, Toussaint told the French government, "Ah, since one reproaches the blacks for throwing out their former tyrants, isn't it part of their duty to prove that they know how to forgive—to welcome the same men that persecuted them?"[3]

For Toussaint, the future of the island and his own people came ahead of any other consideration. When Hédouville realized that he could not influence the general, he resigned and left the island at the end of 1798. Toussaint replaced him with Philippe-Rose Roume de Saint Laurent. A Frenchman, Roume had been a member of the commission that had been sent to Saint-Domingue several years earlier. Later he had married a local mulatto woman, so he was far more acceptable to Toussaint and many of the people on the island.

But in appointing Roume himself, Toussaint had taken on a role usually reserved for the French government. This led the French to believe that Toussaint might be about to proclaim the colony's independence. Toussaint was also handling the foreign affairs of Saint-Domingue, often acting in a way that was not supportive of France. For example, the French knew that Toussaint was dealing with the British, accepting military aid from them. In addition, he had agreed to trade with the United States government led by President John Adams. The United States had become involved in a naval war with France and its colonies and refused to trade with any of them. However, the US Congress decided to make a special exception in the case of Saint-Domingue. This was called "Toussaint's Clause."

There were several reasons for this decision. First, trade with the island had been very profitable for American merchants. In addition, Toussaint agreed that Saint-Domingue would not become a safe harbor for Caribbean pirates who had been attacking American ships. Finally, the Saint-Domingue government agreed not to send its own ships to the United States. Southern slave holders—who ran their own plantations—feared that the revolt on the island might spread to their own slaves. If black crews showed up in southern US ports manning Saint-Domingue ships, southerners feared that they might spread the seeds of rebellion among their slaves.

Although Toussaint's policies did not receive the support of the French government, he tried to reassure them that he did not intend to declare independence. He realized that only France had passed a law proclaiming that all the citizens of Saint-Domingue were equal and that slavery was abolished. Britain, Spain, and the United States all supported slavery. Nevertheless, the French feared that Toussaint was acting like an independent leader. And Britain as well as the United States wanted him to declare his independence from France. But Toussaint was too smart a politician to agree. Instead, he believed that it was in the best interests of Saint-Domingue for him to walk a tightrope between all the major powers.

This was very difficult to do. But Toussaint was a gifted leader, and he knew how to keep all the major powers at least partially satisfied while he pursued a policy that benefited the people of Saint-Domingue.

As leader of Saint-Domingue, Toussaint proved that he was not only a skilled general but a skilled political leader, battling the mulattoes while maintaining diplomatic relations with France, Great Britain, and the United States.

The Ruler of Saint-Domingue

Meanwhile, Toussaint faced an unstable situation inside the colony. The south was controlled by a mulatto leader named André Rigaud. Toussaint and Rigaud did not like or trust each other, and both had no intention of

ANDRÉ RIGAUD

Born in 1761, André Rigaud was a mulatto, the son of a French planter and a female slave who worked on his plantation. Rigaud's father sent him to France where he worked as an apprentice to a goldsmith, learning his trade so he could support himself. Later, Rigaud returned to Saint-Domingue and participated in the movement to change the political situation on the island. Like Vincent Ogé, he supported equal rights for free mulattoes. Following the slave revolt, Rigaud became the commander of an army in the west and south of the island. He was very popular with mulatto planters, who were afraid that the slave rebellion in the north might spread to other parts of the colony. While Rigaud respected Toussaint, he did not intend to take orders from him. Instead, the two army leaders found themselves engaged in a civil war, known as the "War of the Knives," that broke out in 1799.

submitting to the other's military power. Before leaving the island, Hédouville had named Rigaud as the new French representative in the colony. So Hédouville and Rigaud were quite angry when Toussaint had appointed Roume instead. In retaliation, Rigaud ordered his army to take over towns that were supposed to be under Toussaint's authority.

The United States and Great Britain, however, supported Toussaint. British ships unloaded barrels of gunpowder for Toussaint's army at Port-au-Prince. The war between the two local leaders quickly became very brutal. In Cap Français, Toussaint executed more than fifty people who had supported Rigaud, while Rigaud's supporters tried at least three times to assassinate Toussaint. Meanwhile, Toussaint's commander, General Jean-Jacques Dessalines, carried out mass executions in retaliation against those who may have been involved in the assassination attempts.

Finally, late in 1799, Dessalines besieged the key town of Jacmel on the southern coast—a stronghold of Rigaud's forces. The American warship USS *General Greene* helped Dessalines by blockading the town from the ocean. The warship then began bombarding Jacmel, forcing Rigaud's troops to flee along with many of the town's inhabitants. Several months later, in July 1800, Dessalines decisively defeated Rigaud and forced him to flee from Saint-Domingue to France. Soon afterward, Toussaint took over Rigaud's last stronghold at Les Cayes, eastward from Jacmel along the coast.

Toussaint was a religious man who practiced Christianity. Following the victory over Rigaud, he gave thanks to God. "What prayers of thanksgiving, O my God, could be equal to the favor which your divine bounty has just spread out over us," Toussaint said. "Not content to love us, to die for us, to pour out your blood on the cross to buy us out of slavery, you have come once again to overwhelm us with your blessings, and to save us another time."[4]

9

Toussaint Battles Napoleon

Napoleon Bonaparte was born in 1769 on the island of Corsica in the Mediterranean Sea. His father, Carlo, who was a lawyer, and his mother, Letizia, were members of the minor nobility. But the family was not wealthy. Nevertheless, they did have enough money to afford to send Napoleon to school in France, and he graduated from a French military academy in 1785. Napoleon decided to join the artillery, and his career might have followed the normal route of most French artillery officers—slowly moving up through the ranks, finally becoming commanders in charge of an artillery unit. But in 1789, the French Revolution began. And during the early years of the republic, Napoleon helped defend the government against an attack by royalists who supported the monarchy.

In 1796, Napoleon was sent to Italy to defend French interests against the Austrian Empire. In a daring crossing of the Alps during the winter, Napoleon brought his army unexpectedly into Italy where he decisively defeated the Austrians. He was not yet thirty, but already Napoleon had made a name for himself as a brilliant campaigner and a man who was willing to take risks to achieve victory. A year later, he was sent to Egypt to cut off the supply line that England maintained with its empire in India. Once

The battle for Saint-Domingue came down to a titanic struggle between Napoleon Bonaparte and Toussaint L'Ouverture, known as the "Napoleon of Haiti."

again he won an impressive victory—this time against the Egyptian rulers at the Battle of the Pyramids. But a British naval force under the command of Horatio Nelson blockaded the French ships and destroyed them at the Battle of the Nile. Leaving his army behind, Napoleon escaped back to France.

In a coup during 1799, Napoleon overthrew the government of the French Republic. He established himself as the First Consul, the leader of the new government. Then, at the Battle of Marengo in 1800, Napoleon won another brilliant victory against the Austrians. He was cheered by the French who were happy to have the young general run France as a virtual dictator. Napoleon was also committed to rebuilding and expanding the French Empire across Europe and in the New World. This would bring him into direct conflict with Toussaint. And the two gifted generals would become engaged in a battle to the death for control of Saint-Domingue.

A Clash of Giants

Like Napoleon, Toussaint had become a dictator with complete control of Saint-Domingue. He had eliminated his rivals, like Rigaud. He issued the laws, appointed the island's administrators, directed the army, made agreements with foreign powers, and demanded that the former slaves go back to work on the plantations. He had even taken over the former Spanish part of the island. With an army of twenty thousand soldiers, General Moise—one of Toussaint's most successful leaders—rapidly defeated the Spanish in Santo Domingo. Toussaint feared that unless he controlled the entire island of Hispaniola, an invading army might land on the Spanish side and advance toward Saint-Domingue. Toussaint immediately freed all the slaves there. In 1802, when he entered its capital city, Santo Domingo, he received "a tumultuous reception."[1]

Since all of these decisions were made without the permission of the French government, which was led by Napoleon, the First Consul, as he called himself, was not happy about them. But this did not stop Toussaint, who once told his friends, "I felt that I was destined for great things. When I received this divine portent, I was fifty-four years old … The revolution of Saint-Domingue was going its way; I saw that the Whites could not hold out, because they were divided among themselves and crushed by superior numbers; I congratulated myself on being Black."[2] Even at his advanced age, Toussaint showed that he had the energy of a much younger man. He slept only about two hours each night and spent most of the day on horseback or sending out commands through his many secretaries. Now "Old Toussaint," or "Papa Toussaint," as he was known among many of his followers, would face the most severe test of his self-confidence and military expertise.

Napoleon, at age thirty-three, was considered the greatest general in Europe. He was also a dictator who regarded anyone that did not follow his commands as a rebel who had to be destroyed. Until 1802, he had been unable to send a large military force against Saint-Domingue. But in that year, he won decisive military victories against his enemies in Europe and also signed a peace treaty with Great Britain. This meant that the British fleet would not stop him from sending a French army to the Caribbean. Meanwhile, President Thomas Jefferson of the United States also indicated that he would

Napoleon sent a French army under the command of his brother-in-law, General Victor-Emmanuel Leclerc, to Saint-Domingue to destroy Toussaint and his armies.

not supply Toussaint if the French attacked him. Jefferson owned slaves on his plantation in Virginia and did not support the cause of abolition, whether it occurred in the United States or in nearby Saint-Domingue.

Late in 1801, as the peace treaty with Great Britain was about to be signed, Napoleon sent a large expedition to Saint-Domingue. The French force of over twenty thousand soldiers was under the command of General Victor-Emmanuel Leclerc, Napoleon's brother-in-law, married to his sister Pauline. Leclerc was a veteran of battles in Italy, Germany, and Spain, and he had gained Napoleon's confidence. On February 2, 1802, Leclerc's fleet dropped anchor just outside Cap Français. This city, along with Port-au-Prince, was heavily defended by Toussaint's armies. They numbered about the same as the French. In addition, there were armed guerrillas across the island ready to support Toussaint's regular armies.

89

However, when Toussaint saw the large French fleet of sixty-seven ships outside the harbor, he remarked, "We'll all have to die. All France has come to Saint-Domingue."[3] Nevertheless, Toussaint seemed prepared to fight to the death, if necessary, to preserve the island's freedom and the abolition of slavery, if Napoleon and his veteran troops tried to take back control. The French leader regarded blacks as inferior to white French citizens and French soldiers. In a set of secret orders, he had directed General Leclerc to pretend to assure the people of the island that the French meant them no harm. Then Leclerc would demand that Toussaint resign from office, and the French general would take command of the black army. Finally, Leclerc would arrest and execute Toussaint and his commanders.

The Struggle for Hispaniola

The French had hoped to capture Cap Français, but they were to be disappointed. Toussaint left one of his best generals, Henri Christophe, in charge of the city. When Christophe realized that he had too few troops to defend the city against attack, he burned it to the ground, including his own house—the first dwelling he set on fire. Christophe took his army out of Cap Français and disappeared into the mountains to carry out a guerrilla war. Meanwhile, General Dessalines, who had been placed in charge of Port-au-Prince, abandoned the capital and also retreated into the countryside to carry on the war.

Sensing that victory might be near, General Leclerc sent a message to Toussaint calling on him to surrender. The message was carried by Toussaint's two sons, Isaac and Placide. Six years earlier, Toussaint had sent them to

France to be educated. "If General Leclerc really wants peace," Toussaint said to his sons, "let him halt the march of his troops."[4] One of them carried this message back to the French, while the other joined his father's soldiers.

"When you arrive in your country, you will make it known to your father that the French government accords him protection, glory and honor, and that it is not sending an army into the country to battle him, but only to make the French name respected against enemies of the country." —Napoleon Bonaparte[5]

Meanwhile, the war had grown especially vicious. As Dessalines retreated inland, his soldiers massacred hundreds of white plantation owners and townspeople. The French armies were just as brutal, killing innocent black civilians as they marched after Toussaint's forces. Across the northern plains, plantations lay in ruins, and towns had been totally destroyed. This was warfare at its most brutal. Heavy rains in February brought the pace of the war almost to a halt. Nevertheless, French troops under General Donatien Rochambeau—a hero of the American Revolution—continued to chase Toussaint's army.

The two armies fought a bloody battle in late February at Morne Barade, just south of Cap Français. Toussaint had been fortunate to escape with his army, but the French had also failed to win a decisive victory. On February 28, General Dessalines occupied a hill called La Crête-à-Pierrot, south of Morne Barade. A fort had been built there, which was now fortified to defend it against attack. Several French armies soon converged on the position. In the first attacks, led by General Rochambeau and General Debelle, the French were driven back, suffering eight hundred dead and wounded. As a result, the French decided to begin a siege of the fort, hoping to starve out its defenders. Although the French eventually took the town, many of Dessalines's soldiers escaped.

"We surrounded his post with more than twelve thousand men," one French general said later, "he got away without losing half of his garrison, and left us nothing but his dead and his wounded." [6] These soldiers were murdered by Rochambeau. But the war continued, with Toussaint's armies carrying on a continuous guerrilla war against the French troops. Each time they would cross one set of hills, the French would see another row of hills, with more guerrillas shooting at their soldiers. They rolled large boulders across small paths and roads or erected barriers across them with branches. When the French soldiers were forced to halt and clear the areas, black soldiers fired at them from the cover of the trees.

Nevertheless, the relentless French advance had gradually begun having a decisive impact. Toussaint's generals had been growing tired of the war. None of the battles had been decisive, and the French kept on fighting. Some of the black generals also believed Leclerc when he offered them peace if they surrendered along with their forces. General Christophe brought his troops over to the French side in late April as well as all of the towns he had conquered. Others had also agreed to give up the fight. Finally, on May 6, Toussaint rode into Cap Français along with three hundred of his cavalry and surrendered to Leclerc.

WOMEN IN TOUSSAINT'S ARMY

During the wars in Saint-Domingue, women always played important roles. And the war against the French armies was no different. Some women became guerrillas, fighting alongside men in the mountains. This was especially dangerous because they might be ambushed by French troops at almost any time, killed, or captured and then hanged. Others took on the dangerous work of spies. They risked capture by infiltrating the French camps and gathering intelligence about their upcoming movements. Then they carried this information to the black generals, so they could set ambushes for the French troops. Once again, if these women had been caught, they would have been tried and hanged. Women also acted as messengers between black armies, helping Toussaint, Dessalines, and Christophe coordinate their movements. In addition, women often carried food from the countryside to the soldiers in the mountains, enabling them to keep fighting against the French.

"My general," he said, "I am too old and too ill; I need rest to live in the country. I can no longer serve the Republic. I want to go with my children to my plantation at Ennery [southeast of Cap Français.]"[7]

At first, Leclerc agreed to let Toussaint retire. But the French general's orders from Napoleon had been specific, and they did not allow Toussaint to spend his last years in quiet retirement. In June, he was captured near his plantation, put aboard the French ship *L'Héros*, and transported to France. As he left the island for the last time, Toussaint said, "In overthrowing me, you have only cut down the trunk of the tree of liberty of the blacks in Saint-Domingue: it will spring back from the roots, for they are numerous and deep."[8]

Leclerc began to realize that Toussaint was right. Thousands of his men were dying of malaria and yellow fever, decimating his army. And the black guerrillas that had not surrendered to the French kept on fighting. Leclerc wrote to the French government that he could only win by being sent more troops and then by destroying every black on the island, except children under the age of twelve. Unfortunately, Leclerc had contracted yellow fever and was daily growing weaker along with his soldiers. "Sickness is causing frightful havoc in the army under my command," he began. Already "I have at this moment 3,600 men in hospital. For the last 15 days I have been losing from 30 to 50 men a day," Leclerc added. He went on to say that his troops could not put down revolts among the black soldiers. And each day he grew steadily weaker, adding, "I leave this to go back to my bed where I am hoping not to stay too long."[9] But it was already too late for Leclerc to win the victory he desired; soon afterward he died of the yellow fever that had been weakening him for so long. And the war continued without him.

> "My position becomes worse from day to day. I am in such a miserable plight that I have no idea when and how I will get out of it ... I had believed up to the present that the malady would stop ... They tell me today that it will probably last [much longer] ... If that happens and continues with the same intensity the colony will be lost." —General Leclerc to Napoleon[10]

10

The Final Struggle for Freedom

"If I wanted to count all the services of all kinds that I have rendered to the government," Toussaint wrote to Napoleon, "I would need several volumes, and still I wouldn't finish it all. And to compensate me for all these services, they arrested me arbitrarily in Saint-Domingue; they choked me and dragged me on board like a criminal, without any decorum and without any regard for my rank ... Should my conduct make me expect such treatment?"[1]

Toussaint hoped that Napoleon would give him a fair hearing and eventually set him free. But the First Consul had no intention of considering Toussaint's pleas for fairness. He had imprisoned the black leader in the vast medieval castle at Fort de Joux, behind high walls and three moats that encircled the structure. The fort was located in the Jura Mountains, where snow fell eight months of the year—a climate far different from the one on Hispaniola, where Toussaint had lived most of his life. Toussaint was already in his fifties, battle worn and exhausted, and Napoleon expected that he would die

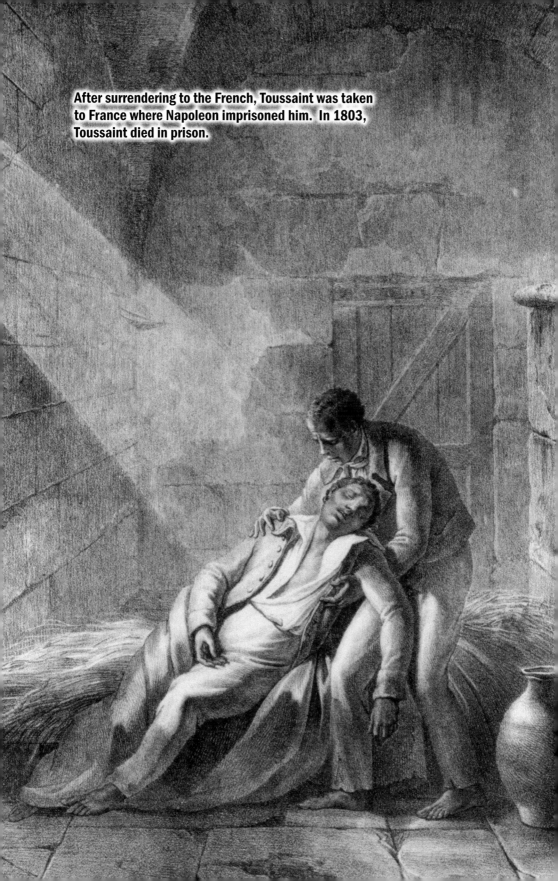

After surrendering to the French, Toussaint was taken to France where Napoleon imprisoned him. In 1803, Toussaint died in prison.

behind bars. As General Leclerc had written Napoleon before his death from yellow fever, "You cannot possibly keep Toussaint at too great a distance … nor put him in a prison too sure; that man has fanaticized this country to such a point that his presence would set it on fire all over again."[2]

Still Toussaint did not give up hope and kept pleading with Napoleon to consider his case. "I hoped … that they would bring me before a tribunal, there to make an account of my conduct, and there to be judged. But far from it … they took me to a fort on the frontiers of the Republic, where they have shut me into a terrible cell … They have sent me to France naked as a worm; they have seized my property and my papers; they have spread the most atrocious calumnies on my account."[3]

Toussaint believed that he had spent most of his time as leader of Saint-Domingue defending the colony from the British and the Spanish. But Napoleon saw things far differently, and he had no intention of putting Toussaint on trial where he might become a martyr to the cause of independence. In addition, Napoleon believed that Toussaint had made a great fortune in gold, which he had buried somewhere near his plantations. He ordered his soldiers to begin hunting for it. No money was ever found, however, and it is most likely that Toussaint and his wife had simply owned several lucrative sugar plantations but very little else. Toussaint had awarded plantations to himself and his generals as the spoils of war.

While Leclerc had promised Toussaint that he would be forgiven for his past activities, the general had lied, instead carrying out the orders of Napoleon. From his prison cell, Toussaint wrote to Napoleon, "If you had no more need of my services and if you wanted to replace

THE WORDS OF WILLIAM WORDSWORTH

Toussaint's fate had not occurred without the notice of the people in Western Europe. In England, the poet William Wordsworth wrote a short poem—titled, simply, "To Toussaint L'Ouverture"—in 1802 dedicated to the revolutionary's life:

> Toussaint, the most unhappy of men!
> Whether the whistling Rustic tend his plough
> Within thy hearing, or thy head by now
> Pillowed in some deep dungeon's earless den;
> O miserable Chieftain! where and when
> Wilt thou find patience? Yet die not; do thou
> Wear rather in thy bonds a cheerful brow:
> Though fallen thyself, never to rise again,
> Live, and take comfort. Thou has left behind
> Powers that will work for thee; air, earth,
>   and skies;
> There's not a breathing of the common wind
> That will forget thee; thou hast great allies;
> Thy friends are exultations, agonies,
> And love, and man's unconquerable mind.[4]

me, shouldn't you have behaved with me as you always behave with regard to white French generals? No doubt I owe this treatment to my color … Does the color of my body tarnish my honor and my courage?"[5]

But Napoleon paid no attention, and in April 1803, Toussaint died in his jail cell from starvation and cold.

The War in Saint-Domingue

Meanwhile, the war in Saint-Domingue continued. Toussaint had predicted that his capture would not bring an end to the fight for independence, and he was right. Although the French forces had been reinforced, most of these troops died from malaria and yellow fever. In May 1802, Napoleon had also announced that the abolition law passed by the French legislature in 1794, during the French Revolution, would be revoked. In colonies like Martinique, which had never abolished slavery, the First Consul ordered that it would continue. And the leaders in Saint-Domingue strongly believed that if the French regained control of their colony, slavery would be reintroduced there, too. Those leaders who had decided to join the French now left and continued their guerrilla war against France. They were joined by the mulatto leaders, who believed that Napoleon would not give them equality with the whites. For the first time, mulatto and black troops were fighting together.

> **"The trade in slaves and their importation into the … colonies will take place in conformity with the law and rules existing before … 1789." —Napoleon[6]**

Toussaint was succeeded by one of his generals, Jean-Jacques Dessalines, who eventually drove the French off the island of Hispaniola and declared himself emperor of Haiti in 1804.

The general in charge of these forces was now Jean-Jacques Dessalines. His leadership was quite different from Toussaint's, who had tried to walk a thin line between the white plantation owners, the mulattoes, and the blacks. It was a balanced, subtle policy that Toussaint believed was essential to rebuilding the economy after the war had ended. As historian C. L. R. James wrote, "Dessalines was a one-sided genius, but he was the man for this crisis, not Toussaint. He gave blow for blow." General Rochambeau, who took over command of the French army from Leclerc, "put to death 500 at [the battle around] Le Cap [Français] and buried them in a large hole dug while they waited for execution … Dessalines raised gibbets of branches and hanged 500 for Rochambeau and the whites of Le Cap to see."[7] In short, the brutality of the war reached extremes that had never been seen before.

One French observer wrote, referring to the black soldiers, "What men these blacks are! How they fight and how they die! One has to make war against them to know their reckless courage in braving danger … The more they fell, the greater seemed to be the courage of the rest."[8]

Dessalines realized that to preserve Saint-Domingue, the French had to be forced out and independence declared. Meanwhile, war between Britain and France had resumed in 1803, so Napoleon realized he could not enforce General Rochambeau's army. Recognizing that he would not achieve victory, Rochambeau massacred many of the blacks and mulattoes—men, women, and children—whom he had captured. Dessalines retaliated by killing French civilians. In October, the French left their stronghold at Port-au-Prince and retreated toward Cap Français. Outside the city, Dessalines decisively defeated them at the Battle of Vertières. Rochambeau

CRY OF BATTLE

Advancing into battle against the French grenadiers and their artillery, Dessalines's soldiers were brutal in their attacks and unsparing in their desire to kill the French. The bloody war against the French was reflected in a song sung by the black soldiers:

> *To the attack, grenadier,*
> *Who gets killed, that's his affair.*
> *Forget your ma,*
> *Forget your pa,*
> *To the attack, grenadier,*
> *Who gets killed, that's his affair.* [9]

In 1804, Dessalines would issue a decree to kill all the French people who remained on the island and his reputation as one of the most ruthless and brutal rulers in the world was cemented.

surrendered to Dessalines and left the island. Behind him, fifty thousand French troops had died in Napoleon's attempt to retake Saint-Domingue.

As Napoleon later wrote: "I have to reproach myself for the attempt at the colony ... it was a great mistake to have wanted to subdue it by force; I should have contented myself to govern it through the intermediary of Toussaint."[10]

As a result of losing Haiti, Napoleon gave up his dream of a French empire in the western hemisphere and sold a large piece of territory, known as the Louisiana Purchase, to the United States.

The Results of Victory

Napoleon's defeat had far-reaching consequences in the Caribbean and North America. He had hoped to reassert the strength of the French Empire in the New World, but his loss of Saint-Domingue changed all his plans. That empire was supposed to include part of North America, although he would soon lose the last of French territory there when he sold it off under the Louisiana Purchase.

The political situation in Saint-Domingue changed, too. On January 1, 1804, Dessalines announced that the country would now be called Haiti. This was a name given to the island of Hispaniola by the Taino Indians, the original inhabitants. Dessalines also announced the independence of Haiti from France. During February and March 1804, Dessalines ordered the massacre of all white men, women, and children remaining in the new nation. He also required

THE LOUISIANA PURCHASE

In North America, the French controlled the Louisiana territory, a vast piece of land of approximately 800,000 square miles (2,071,990 sq km) stretching westward from New Orleans and across the Mississippi River. With the loss of Saint-Domingue, however, Napoleon offered this vast tract of land to the United States for only $15 million. In 1803, President Thomas Jefferson agreed to buy the property—the Louisiana Purchase—changing the entire course of American history by more than doubling the size of the United States. The agreement between France and the United States said, in part,

The First Consul of the French Republic desiring to give to the United States a strong proof of his friendship, doth hereby cede to the said United States, in the name of the French Republic, forever and in full sovereignty, the said territory, with all its rights and appurtenances as fully and in the same manners as they have been acquired by the French Republic.[11]

that blacks continue working on the plantations, whether they liked it or not, to ensure the revival of the Haitian economy. Finally, in 1804, Dessalines declared himself the emperor of Haiti—much like Napoleon who had become emperor of France that same year.

Emperor Dessalines established an autocratic state, like Napoleon's France. The war that won the nation's independence had cost the island one-third of its population, over 100,000 people. It also established a tradition of dictatorship in Haiti that lasted for almost two centuries.

CONCLUSION

The life of Toussaint L'Ouverture points out how difficult political leadership can be. Toussaint led an independence movement, much like George Washington in the United States had done. But the movement in Haiti took a very different turn. Part of that was probably due to the man who led it, and part was due to the circumstances and the history of the people whom he led to independence.

Great leaders are often complex personalities. Thomas Jefferson, for example, wrote the Declaration of Independence, but he was also a slaveholder in Virginia. Napoleon Bonaparte fought under the French flag, which was a symbol of liberty, equality, and fraternity, but he was also a dictator who crowned himself French emperor in 1804.

Toussaint was no different. He fought for the freedom of more than 250,000 slaves who worked the plantations in Saint-Domingue. But once they were freed, he required them to go back to work on the sugar and coffee plantations. He recognized that without successful plantations that provided crops that could be exported for money, Saint-Domingue could not survive. The free blacks resented him for this decision, but Toussaint ignored their feelings because he believed that he knew what was best for Saint-Domingue.

Toussaint recognized that the British wanted to continue slavery in all of their colonies in the Caribbean. Nevertheless, he also knew that England was the enemy of France so he made an alliance with the British—who had the world's strongest navy—to cut French supply lines

Toussaint L'Ouverture was a complex and highly gifted leader who led the only successful slave revolt in world history.

from Europe. He recognized that without supplies the French army could be defeated.

Toussaint was also willing to work with the white plantation owners, although they were hated by the former slaves. He knew that these owners were the only ones who could run the plantations—the foundation of the Saint-Domingue economy. So he tried to get along with them, and he even relied on some of them as his advisors.

While Toussaint could forgive those who had fought against him, like the whites and the mulattoes, he could also be brutal in putting down revolts. Some of his brutality took the form of mass executions that included men, women, and children. He also treated some of the captured French soldiers savagely to make examples of them so their leaders might recognize that they could not defeat the black armies.

At the same time, Toussaint showed great restraint in his treatment of some whites on the island. He defended the wife of his employer on the Breda plantation and ensured her safety. Toussaint also brought a group of white prisoners to safety in Cap Français. Thus, Toussaint was a complicated figure, much like other human beings. While working for a society free of a rigid class structure, he also dressed in fine uniforms, owned several plantations, and ruled as a dictator.

Toussaint proved himself a practical, skilled politician and military leader. Having learned how to read and write at a young age, Toussaint read widely, learning about military strategy and political leadership. He also mastered the skills of animal medicine and gained great respect as a military doctor.

Even in his fifties he seemed inexhaustible, working almost around the clock, traveling miles each day to inspect his troops and their fortifications and dictating endless reports to his secretaries. He showed himself to be a tireless leader, the type that is often needed to create a new country.

Toussaint was guided by his beliefs: a strong Catholicism, a love of Saint-Domingue, and a commitment to provide freedom for all the slaves on the island. To accomplish this goal, he was willing to take on the world's most powerful army and perhaps its most gifted military leader—Napoleon—to achieve victory. There were many times when this victory seemed impossible, the odds against Toussaint too great, and the armies that opposed him too large. Nevertheless, he never lost faith in himself or in his cause, and he finally established a new nation.

Unfortunately, that nation achieved complete independence without him. And it quickly fell under the domination of a ruthless dictator. This established a precedent that continued in Haiti for the next two hundred years. Haiti endured violence, its economy declined, and today it is one of the world's poorest nations. Revolutions that begin with a great desire for liberty and a willingness for people to sacrifice their lives to achieve freedom can take a wrong turn. The French Revolution led to the dictatorship of Napoleon and the establishment of a European empire. The Russian Revolution of 1917 began with the overthrow of an autocratic Tsar but ended with an even more brutal dictatorship by the communists.

One of the few exceptions has been the American Revolution. It began with a call for liberty and continued with a freely elected democratic government that has flourished into the twenty-first century.

CHRONOLOGY

1739–1746 The probable period of Toussaint's birth.

1769 Napoleon Bonaparte is born in Corsica.

1772 Toussaint becomes a coachman and chief assistant on the Breda plantation.

1777 Toussaint is freed by the plantation manager.

1782 Toussaint marries Suzanne Simone Baptiste; they have three sons.

1788 Louis XVI calls the Estates-General to meet for the first time since 1614.

1789 The French Revolution begins; the Bastille is stormed by a French mob; the National Assembly passes the Declaration of the Rights of Man.

1790 Vincent Ogé launches a revolution in Saint-Domingue and the Colonial Assembly is established in Saint-Domingue.

1791 A slave revolt erupts in Saint-Domingue, and Toussaint becomes a leader of the revolt.

1792 The Colonial Assembly refuses to make peace with Toussaint.

1793 The French government executes King Louis XVI; the revolutionary government sends the First Commission to Saint-Domingue; the commissioners lead an attack on Port-au-Prince; blacks attack and burn Cap Français; the commission announces the end to slavery in Saint-Domingue; the British invade Saint-Domingue.

1794 France abolishes slavery in its empire; Queen Marie Antoinette is executed.

1795 Toussaint agrees to work with the French Republic and becomes the most important black leader in Saint-Domingue.

1796 The French send the Second Commission to Saint-Domingue; Napoleon defeats the Austrians.

1797 The British withdraw troops from Saint-Domingue.

1798 Toussaint is the undisputed leader of Saint-Domingue, although it remains a French colony.

1799 Toussaint and mulatto leader André Rigaud begin the War of the Knives; Napoleon becomes First Consul of France.

1800 Rigaud is decisively defeated and leaves Saint-Domingue.

1801 France and Great Britain sign a peace treaty; Napoleon invades Saint-Domingue.

1802 Toussaint takes control of the Spanish colony of Santo Domingo on Hispaniola; a French fleet arrives at Cap Français; French and Toussaint's forces fight bloody battles for control of Saint-Domingue; Napoleon announces that slavery will be restored in the French Empire; French General Leclerc and many of his soldiers die of malaria and yellow fever; Toussaint is captured and imprisoned in France.

1803 Toussaint dies in French prison; General Jean-Jacques Dessalines leads the black army to victory over the French; Napoleon sells Louisiana Territory to the United States for $15 million.

1804 Dessalines becomes emperor of an independent Haiti.

Chapter Notes

Chapter 1. The Black Spartacus

1. C. L. R. James, *The Black Jacobins* (New York: Random House, 1989), p. 25.

Chapter 2. Toussaint and Saint-Domingue

1. C. L. R. James, *The Black Jacobins* (New York: Vintage Books, 1963), p. 17.

2. James, pp. 7–8.

3. Peter Kolchin, *American Slavery: 1619-1877* (New York: Hill and Wang, 1993), p. 21.

4. "The Code Noir (The Black Code)," Liberty, Equality, Fraternity: Exploring the French Revolution, *Roy Rosenzweig Center for History and New Media.* Accessed February 9, 2017, https://chnm.gmu.edu /revolution/d/335.

5. James, pp. 45, 55.

6. James, p. 12.

7. Madison Smartt Bell, *Toussaint Louverture: A Biography* (New York: Pantheon Books, 2007), p. 59.

8. Bell, pp. 64–65.

Chapter 3. Big Whites and Small Whites

1. C. L. R. James, *The Black Jacobins* (New York: Random House, 1989), p. 41.

2. James, p. 43.

3. James, p. 33.

4. James, p. 45.

5. James, p. 55.

6. James, p. 17.

7. James, p. 10.

Chapter 4. Winds of Change

1. C. L. R. James, *The Black Jacobins* (New York: Random House, 1989), p. 60.

Chapter 5. Slave Revolt in Saint-Domingue

1. "Tacky's Rebellion," *Caribya*, http://caribya.com /jamaica/history/tackys.rebellion.

2. Jeremy D. Popkin, *A Concise History of the Haitian Revolution* (Oxford, England: Wiley-Blackwell, 2012), p. 38.

3. Popkin, pp. 38, 39.

4. Madison Smartt Bell, *Toussaint Louverture: A Biography* (New York: Pantheon Books, 2007), p. 23.

5. Bell, p. 28.

Chapter 6. 1793–1794

1. Madison Smartt Bell, *Toussaint Louverture: A Biography* (New York: Pantheon Books, 2007), p. 33.

2. Bell., p. 93.

3. Bell, p. 47.

4. Bell, p. 113.

5. Bell, p. 91.

Chapter 7. Slaves No More

1. Madison Smartt Bell, *Toussaint Louverture: A Biography* (New York: Pantheon Books, 2007), p. 104.

2. Jeremy D. Popkin, *A Concise History of the Haitian Revolution* (Oxford, England: Wiley-Blackwell, 2012), p. 71.

3. Popkin, p. 72.

4. Popkin, p. 80.

5. Popkin, p. 88.

Chapter 8. Toussaint in Power

1. Jeremy D. Popkin, *A Concise History of the Haitian Revolution* (Oxford, England: Wiley-Blackwell, 2012), p. 88.

2. C. L. R. James, *The Black Jacobin* (New York: Random House, 1989), p. 205.

3. James, pp. 205–206.

4. Madison Smartt Bell, *Toussaint Louverture: A Biography* (New York: Pantheon Books, 2007), p. 162.

Chapter 9. Toussaint Battles Napoleon

1. Madison Smartt Bell, *Toussaint Louverture: A Biography* (New York: Pantheon Books, 2007), p. 186.

2. Jeremy D. Popkin, *A Concise History of the Haitian Revolution* (Oxford, England: Wiley-Blackwell, 2012), p. 107.

3. Bell, p. 193.

4. Popkin, pp. 118–119.

5. Bell, p. 238.

6. Popkin, p. 124.

7. Bell, p. 252.

8. Bell, p. 265.

9. C. L. R. James, *The Black Jacobin* (New York: Random House, 1989), pp. 330, 349.

10. James, pp. 349–350.

Chapter 10. The Final Struggle for Freedom

1. Madison Smartt Bell, *Toussaint Louverture: A Biography* (New York: Pantheon Books, 2007), p. 261.

2. Bell, p. 267.

3. Ibid.

4. William Wordsworth, "390. To Toussaint L'Ouverture," *Bartleby*. Accessed February 9, 2017, http://www.bartleby.com/41/390.html.

5. Bell, p. 268.

6. Bell, p. 285.

7. Bell, p. 276.

8. C. L. R. James, *The Black Jacobin* (New York: Random House, 1989), p. 361.

9. James, p. 368.

10. Ibid.

11. "Treaty With France (Louisiana Purchase)," 1803, *Bartleby*. Accessed February 9, 2017, http://www.bartleby.com/43/25.html.

GLOSSARY

big whites Upper-class white plantation owners in Saint-Domingue; known as *grande blancs* in French.

Black Code Laws that white plantation owners followed to govern black slaves in the French Empire; known as *Le Code Noir* in French.

exclusive A colonial system requiring French colonies to trade only with France.

free blacks Slaves who had been freed by their masters.

Haiti An indigenous Taino word that became the name of the independent nation of Saint-Domingue.

Hispaniola The large Caribbean island that Christopher Columbus visited in 1492 and which contained the French colony Saint-Domingue and the Spanish colony Santo Domingo; Hispaniola now contains the countries of Haiti and the Dominican Republic.

Louisiana Purchase The name for the purchase of 800,000 square miles (2,071,990 sq km) of French territory in North America by the United States in 1803.

Maroons Escaped slaves who lived as free people in the mountains of Saint-Domingue.

Middle Passage The voyage that took slaves from Africa to the New World.

mulattoes Free mixed-race people, typically born of a white father and a black mother or two mixed-race parents.

Saint-Domingue The French colony on the island of Hispaniola, which is now the country of Haiti.

Santo Domingo The Spanish colony on the island of Hispaniola, which is now the Dominican Republic.

small whites White professionals and merchants in Saint-Domingue; known as *petits blancs* in French.

Spartacus A slave leader in ancient Rome.

tight packers Slave ships that carried as many slaves as possible in their holds to increase their profit.

voodoo The native religion of blacks on Saint-Domingue.

War of the Knives The civil war that began in 1799 between blacks and mulattoes.

FURTHER READING

Books

Girard, Phillipe. *The Memoir of General Toussaint Louverture*. New York: Oxford University Press, 2014.

Girard, Phillipe. *Toussaint Louverture: A Revolutionary Life*. New York: Basic Books, 2016.

Parkinson, Wenda. *This Gilded African: Toussaint L'Ouverture*. New York: HBC Communications, 2015.

Rockwell, Anne. *Open the Door to Liberty! A Biography of Toussaint L'Ouverture*. New York: Houghton Mifflin, 2009.

Websites

Brown University Library: The History of Haiti (1492–1805)
library.brown.edu/haitihistory
This website offers a chronology of events throughout the history of Haiti, including photographs, engravings, and primary source documents.

French Empire Biographies
frenchempire.net/biographies
This website provides information on leaders of the French Empire throughout the world from the 1600s through the 1900s, including Toussaint L'Ouverture.

Films

Haitian Revolution: Toussaint L'Ouverture, 2009
This hour-long documentary examines the life of L'Ouverture and the history of the Haitian Revolution.

Toussaint Louverture, 2012
A French film, written and directed by Phillipe Niang, that profiles the great Haitian revolutionary.

INDEX

A

Adams, John, 76
Akwamu, 46

B

Baptiste, Pierre, 25
Baptiste, Suzanne Simone (wife), 24
Bastille Day, 41
Biassou, Georges, 20, 24–25, 51–52, 62, 110
Billet, Jeannot, 49
Black Code, 8, 21–22, 24, 46, 56
Black Jacobins, The, 19
Bleigeat, Marie Eugenie, 71
Bonaparte, Napoleon
    rise to power, 84–86
    Saint-Domingue, 87–107
Breda plantation, 25

C

Caesar, Julius, 62, 63
Cap Français, 20, 25, 32, 33, 49, 51–54, 57, 61, 70, 74, 83, 89–92, 94, 102, 110

Caribbean, 7, 8, 12, 15, 20, 46, 56, 78, 80, 87, 105, 108
Christianity, 16, 49, 77, 83
Christophe, Henri, 90–93
Colonial Assembly, 38, 41, 45, 57
Columbus, Christopher, 7, 8, 15, 20
Crassus, Marcus Licinius, 12
Cudjoe, 48

D

Declaration of the Rights of Man, 42, 43
Dessalines, Jean-Jacques, 83, 90–93, 101–103, 105, 107
dictatorship, 86, 87, 107, 108, 110, 11
Dutty, Boukman, 49, 52, 55

E

Estates-General, 38–39, 41
executions, 40, 45, 64, 83, 102, 110

F

financial crisis, 38

First Consul, 86, 87, 96, 100, 106

Fort de Joux, 96

French army, 12, 22, 40, 59–61, 64–65, 71, 75, 78, 82, 84, 86–88, 90–91, 93–94, 102, 110–111

French Republic, 12, 58, 60–62, 70, 73, 78, 84, 86, 94, 106

French Revolution, 39–40, 42–43, 45, 58, 64, 66, 69, 73, 84, 87, 91, 100, 111–112

G

Gaou-Guinou, 20, 24

General Greene, 83

Girod-Chantrans, Justin, 35

Great Britain, 34, 38, 64, 81, 83, 87, 89, 102

guerrilla tactics, 53, 89–90, 92–94, 100

H

Haiti, 105, 107, 108, 111

Hédouville, Joseph, 76, 78–79, 82

Hispaniola, 7, 8, 15, 20, 60, 77, 86, 90, 96, 101, 105

I

independence, 38, 41, 45, 79, 80, 98, 100, 102, 105, 107, 108, 111

J

Jamaica, 8, 48, 56, 73

Jefferson, Thomas, 106

Jura Mountains, 96

L

Laveaux, Étienne, 59, 61, 67, 71, 73

Leclerc, Victor-Emmanuel, 88–92, 94–95, 98, 102

Libertat, Bayon de, 25–26, 51–53

Libertat, Madame de, 51–52

Louis XVI, 38, 43, 58, 64

Louisiana Purchase, 104–106

L'Ouverture, Isaac (son), 25, 90–91

L'Ouverture, Placide (son), 25, 90–91

L'Ouverture, Toussaint
childhood, 24–28
heritage, 20–24
imprisonment, 96–100
leader, 63–95
legacy, 108–111

role in revolution, 56–75

M
Machiavelli, Niccolo, 23, 25
malaria, 22, 34, 64, 70, 94, 100
Marie Antoinette, 58, 64
Maroons, 46, 48, 49, 56, 58
Marthe, Louis, 43
Mediterranean Sea, 12, 84
mercantile system, 34, 39
Mezy, Lenormand de, 49
Mirabeau, Honoré, 41, 43
mosquitoes, 12, 64
mulattoes, 28–29, 31, 39, 40, 42, 44, 55, 60, 70–71, 79–82, 100, 102, 110

N
National Assembly, 40, 41, 43, 45

O
Ogé, Vincent, 40, 44, 45, 82

P
Papillon, Jean-François, 49, 65
Petite Cormier, 26

plantation owners, 7–8, 21–22, 24–26, 28–31, 35–36, 40, 46, 48–52, 54–56, 58, 62, 64, 70, 78, 91, 102, 110
Polverel, Étienne, 63
Port-au-Prince, 34, 56, 60, 64, 71, 76, 83, 89, 90, 102
Providence Hospital, 25

R
Raimond, Julien, 40, 43
Rigaud, André, 55, 70, 81–83, 86
Rochambeau, Donatien, 91–92, 102
Roume, Philippe-Rose, 79, 82

S
Saint-Domingue
  government, 33–37
  slavery, 37
  society, 29–33
Saint-Domingue revolt
  British forces, 64–65
  eruption, 49–53
  other revolts, 46–49
  Spanish forces, 58–61
  spread, 53–56
  Toussaint's role, 56–57, 68
  victories, 61–62

Santo Domingo, 15, 20, 56, 86–87

Slave Code of 1733, 46

slave songs, 36

Sodtmann, Johannes, 46

Sonthonax, Léger-Félicité, 58, 60–61, 65, 71, 73

South Carolina, 56

Spanish army, 59, 60, 65, 68, 86

Spartacus, 10, 12–13

St. John, 46

T

Tacky, 48

"To Toussaint L'Ouverture," 99

"Toussaint's Clause," 79

U

United States, 26, 56, 79–81, 83, 87, 89, 104, 106, 108

V

Vertières, Battle of, 102

Vesuvius, Mount, 10

Villette, Jean-Louis, 70–71

voodoo, 49, 77

W

women, 93

Wordsworth, William, 99

Y

yellow fever, 22, 34, 64, 70, 94–95, 98, 100